Shakespeare Performances in Japan

Intercultural-Multilingual-Translingual

Emi Hamana

Shumpusha

Shakespeare Performances in Japan:
Intercultural – Multilingual – Translingual

Emi Hamana

2019

Shumpusha

Table of Contents

Acknowledgements ··· 6

Introduction ··· 7

Part I Intercultural and Multilingual Performance ································ 19

Chapter 1 This Is, and Is Not, Shakespeare:
A Japanese-Korean Transformation of *Othello* ································ 21
1. The Critical Impact of Local Shakespeare on Global Shakespeare:
Othello in the Japanese *Mugen* Noh Style with Elements of Korean
Shamanism: A Creative Subversion ·· 24
2. The Critical Impact of the Japanese-Korean Adaptation of *Othello* on
Global Shakespeare ··· 29
 2.1. Translation Matters ·· 29
 2.2. Intercultural Performance Matters ···································· 31

Chapter 2 Performing Shakespeare after the 11 March 2011 Disaster:
Yamanote Jijosha's *The Tempest* ·· 37
1. *The Tempest* as Prospero's Apocalyptic Delusion ····························· 41
2. Caliban's Binding and Torture on Stage ···································· 46
3. An Additional Japanese Ending ··· 47

Chapter 3 The Last Shakespeare Plays Directed by Yukio Ninagawa:
Possessed by the Power of Theatre ··· 53
1. *Richard II* with Wheelchairs and the Tango ································· 57
2. *NINAGAWA (or Samurai) Macbeth*: The Legendary Production Revived ········ 60
3. *The Two Gentlemen of Verona* with an All-Male Cast ························ 63

3

Chapter 4 Multilingual Performances of Shakespeare Worldwide: Multilingual *King Lear*, Directed by Tadashi Suzuki ··············· 67
1. Tadashi Suzuki and Multilingual Performance ·· 69
2. A Short Performance History of *King Lear* (1984–2006), Directed by Tadashi Suzuki ·· 71
3. The Four-Language Performance of *King Lear* (2009) ···························· 73
3.1. Multilingual Theatre in Singapore with a Focus on Kuo Pao Kun ············· 75
3.2. The Four-Language Version of *King Lear*: Towards a Horizon of Linguistic Break-Up ·· 77

Part II Translingual Performance ·· 87

Chapter 5 Translingual Performances of Shakespeare Worldwide with a Focus on *Henry V* ··· 89
1. Fundamental Concepts and Facts ·· 91
1.1. What is Translingual Practice? ··· 91
1.2. What Are Contact Zones and Contact Languages? ···································· 94
1.3. A Brief Survey of the History of the English Language ···························· 95
1.4. Worldwide Shakespeare Performances in the Age of Global English ············· 96
1.5. London during Shakespeare's Time ·· 97
1.6. Foreigners and Foreign Languages in Shakespeare's Works ···················· 98
2. An Analysis of *Henry V*, Act 5, Scene 2 ·· 103
2.1. *Henry V* as the Most Babylonian Text of Shakespeare's Plays ···················· 103
2.2. The Wooing Scene in *Henry V*, Act 5, Scene 2 ··· 105
2.3. Allocation of Speeches in *Henry V*, Act 5, Scene 2 ··································· 106
2.4. Translingual Practice: Example 1 ·· 107
2.5. Translingual Practice: Example 2 ·· 108
2.6. English-French Connection ·· 112

Chapter 6 *Lear Dreaming*, Directed by Ong Keng Sen ··········· 115
   1. Basic Ideas of *Lear Dreaming* ··········· 118
   2. An Analysis of Several Scenes in *Lear Dreaming* from a Translingual
      Perspective ··········· 123
      2.1. Semiotic Resources ··········· 123
      2.2. Ecological Affordances ··········· 125

Chapter 7 *Safaring the Night: A Midsummer Night's Dream* Updated ··········· 131
   1. Basic Information about *Safaring the Night* ··········· 132
   2. An Analysis of Several Elements of *Safaring the Night*
      from a Translingual Perspective ··········· 138
      2.1. Semiotic Resources ··········· 138
      2.2. Ecological Affordances ··········· 141

Conclusion ··········· 149

Appendix: Performance Review: *Sandaime Richard,* written by Hideki Noda
      and directed by Ong Keng Sen. Performed in Japanese, English and
      Indonesian, with Japanese and English Subtitles. ··········· 153
Notes ··········· 157
Works Cited ··········· 165
List of Original Publications ··········· 177
Author Profile ··········· 179
Index ··········· 181

Acknowledgements

I owe a debt of gratitude to many international institutions, conferences and scholars for helping to assemble this collection of essays since earlier versions of six of the seven chapters were first published. Moreover, I am very grateful for all the constructive comments and encouragement provided by the peer reviewers and editors of the publications in which they first appeared.

The publication of this book is supported by the Academic Society of Tokyo Woman's Christian University. I am immensely grateful for the reviewers' insightful comments and encouragement.

Introduction

The Purpose of this Book

This book is the result of three research projects: the Intercultural Performances of Shakespeare's Plays, Intercultural Education through World Shakespeare Performances and Translingual Performances of Shakespeare Worldwide. Although these projects were closely related and built upon one another, this book is divided into two parts— Part I: Intercultural and Multilingual Performance and Part II: Translingual Performance— according to the order of their development, logical continuity and coherence. The outcomes of the critical explorations presented in Part I lead to the proposal of a challenging new field in Part II, set against the backdrop of a paradigm shift in language education and new approaches in theatre studies.

Part I is concerned with the first and second research projects. The first was a study of the intercultural performances of Shakespeare's plays with the aim of finding model case material for promoting intercultural understanding. Intercultural performance is based on the phenomenon of interculturalism. We are now approaching an age of intercultural performance in which people can live together, not merely accepting or tolerating but understanding (and ideally integrating) the vast cultural differences and diversities found in our increasingly divided globe, even if extremely serious difficulties remain, and thus develop intercultural sensitivity.

Applying theories and methods of postcolonialism and cultural studies, Shakespearean scholars in Eastern Asia have been developing a new field of Shakespeare studies. Their work has attracted the attention of European and American scholars, and they are now expected to develop it further. While on the one hand this book contributes to this research trend, on the other it tries to explore, from a unique vantage point, the intercultural performances of Shakespeare's plays that contribute to promoting intercultural integration.

Although a surge of interest in intercultural communication has recently occurred among Shakespearean scholars, it is not yet at all adequate. While they are certainly interested in intercultural performances, many scholars remain sceptical with regard to the promotion of mutual understanding or find it irrelevant. Many researches are concerned with how Shakespeare's plays are performed on local stages from a disciplinary perspective; however, I argue that the promotion of intercultural sensitivity is vital for the symbiosis of people in our divided world, regardless of the difficulty of promoting intercultural sensitivity.

In this study, I connect intercultural communication studies to drama and performance studies. Many theatre scholars are intent on transmitting their own cultures to a target culture but are less aware of the importance of intercultural sensitivity, which is a vital concept in intercultural communication. Therefore, the purpose of this study is to examine a variety of performance styles used around the world to stage Shakespeare's plays from the perspective of intercultural sensitivity and to identify model performances. If I were a theatre practitioner, I could make a model production myself; as I am not, all I can do as a theatre scholar is to seek out model material and engage in a critical and useful investigation of it.

This study connects two academic fields that have separate origins. One is Shakespeare studies, with its centuries-old tradition, and the other is intercultural communication studies, a field that has made rapid progress as a result of the expansion of globalisation and multiculturalism since the late twentieth century. It aims at exploring model material for the intercultural performance of Shakespeare's plays to promote cultural understanding.

The second research project examined in Part I was a study of intercultural education through theatre and performance studies, with a special focus on world Shakespeare performances, including translations and adaptations of his work (which have been called "tradaptations"). I began the project combining Shakespeare studies and intercultural education more than fifteen years ago, attempting to build a foundation from which to explore world Shakespeare performances and contribute to intercultural education in terms of both theory and practice. The specific aim was to find inspiring performances.

World Shakespeare performance studies and intercultural education studies have been thriving—separately—both in Japan and abroad. By working comprehensively on these subjects, I found myself a pioneer in the field. As economic and cultural globalisation continues apace, it is vital to facilitate intercultural education through world Shakespeare performances and equally important for Japanese researchers to explore it with vigour and make the results of their studies known to the international community.

The World Shakespeare Congress has been concerned with a variety of Shakespeare performances around the globe since its foundation in 1971. World Shakespeare as a discipline has become firmly established since then, and researchers in Europe, the United States and Asia have promoted it. The result has been a wide range of books, papers and websites: examples include the work of Sonia Massai as the editor of *World-Wide Shakespeares* (2005) and Richard Fotheringham et al., who edited *Shakespeare's World/World Shakespeares* (2008). In 2010, with the aim of correcting the prevailing Euro-American centrism in Shakespeare studies, an East Asian research team began to make public the Asian Shakespeare Intercultural Archive (A|S|I|A), a digital archive of Asian Shakespeare performances with subtitles in English, Chinese, Japanese and Korean.

Although the decreasing number of theatregoers due to the rise of internet culture is a matter of serious concern, theatre differs from digital culture or virtual reality; it is a dynamic art form that relies on the interaction between the players and the audience. Its greatest strength is that flesh-and-blood actors are on stage while the audience, making the best use of their imagination, commits itself to the world the players inhabit, living vicariously through that (re)presented world. The power of theatre lies in the fact that the players and the audience build a unique space together while sparking the imagination and disseminating creativity.

Intercultural education aims to relativise our ethnocentric values to make us fully aware of the differences and diversity of culture, language, race, ethnicity and religion and to enhance our ability to live together by adapting to and integrating our cultural differences. As Figure 1 shows, this innovative interdisciplinary study aims to achieve the best results by combining three vital fields.

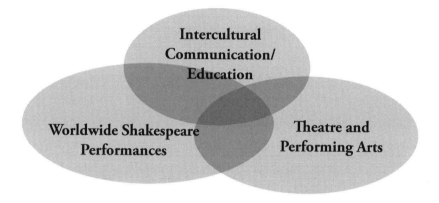

Figure 1: A Conceptual Map of Part I of this Research

The second project connects three academic fields that developed separately. The first is Shakespeare performance studies, the second theatre studies and the third intercultural education. This second project aims to uncover new significance with regard to performing Shakespeare plays and explore theoretical and practical methods to contribute to the promotion of intercultural education that the world requires, an aim that is shared by the first project addressed in Part I.

Part II is concerned with the third research project, which is on translingual performances of Shakespeare worldwide, with a special focus on translingual practice, a part of communication studies and language education studies that is emerging in multilingual nations and regions around the world and a new academic field that has rarely been discussed in Japan. I have explored translingual performances of Shakespeare around the globe and their challenges and possibilities in terms of both theory and practice. The specific aim of this project was to discover inspiring performances and to make effective suggestions for translingual performances of Shakespeare worldwide.

As Suresh Canagarajah points out in *Translingual Practice: Global Englishes and Cosmopolitan Relations* (2013), the term "translingual" emphasises two key concepts that create a paradigm shift in language education. First, "communication transcends individual languages"; second, "communication transcends words and involves diverse semiotic resources [e.g., symbols, icons and images] and environmental affordances" (6). Multilingualism tends to emphasise the coexistence of several languages while slighting their dynamic interaction. A study in translingual practice, by contrast, emphasises the contact between languages and the translingual reality in which we live. It expects not only that translingual performance will represent our translingual reality on the stage, but also that it will represent, create and evoke a deeper reality than that of which we are usually aware.

As mentioned above, the World Shakespeare Congress has examined a variety of Shakespeare performances around the globe. The United Kingdom, the traditional home of Shakespeare productions, invites theatre groups, directors and actors from all over the world to appreciate their productions, thus making Shakespeare more global, and two key events and realisations informed this project and thus this book. First, I watched part of Globe to Globe 2012: Shakespeare's 37 Plays in 37 Languages, a special theatre event held during the London Olympics. I was overwhelmed by this unprecedented display of multilingual and multicultural performances. Second, I realised that I could uncover new significance and possibilities for multilingual performances by employing the concept of translingual practice.

Therefore, this study synergistically connects three vital academic fields that have developed separately (Figure 2). The first is worldwide Shakespeare performance studies, the second is theatre and performing arts studies and the third is the study of translingual practice. It aims to uncover new significance for performing Shakespeare plays and to explore theoretical and practical methods to promote the translingual practice the world requires.

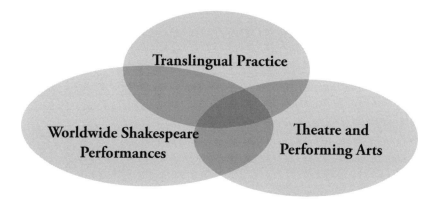

Figure 2: A Conceptual Map of Part II of this Research

A brief survey of this book

This book is composed of seven chapters, four in Part I and three in Part II. As noted above, my projects were aimed at finding and critically investigating new intercultural, multilingual and translingual performances of worldwide Shakespeare. Although I tried to select the most interesting performances within my financial, temporal and linguistic means, the seven chapters are more or less case studies, most of which involve performances in Japan. However, this does not at all suggest that the book aims to consider Shakespeare performances in Japan in a limited sense. It aims to investigate them against the broad background of world Shakespeare performance studies. In fact, all but one chapter deal with international collaborations (Chapters 1 and 6), internationally famous directors' works (Chapters 3, 4 and 6) and works performed by internationally active Japanese theatre companies (Chapters 2 and 7).

Chapter 1 addresses the critical impact of local Shakespeare on global Shakespeare by examining a Japanese-Korean intercultural performance of *Othello* (2008). Incorporating elements of Korean shamanistic ritual and elements from Japanese Noh to create a new reading of Shakespeare's play with a special emphasis on Desdemona's soul, the interaction of the two forms of theatre is powerful. Local Shakespeare functions as a cultural catalyst for two nations vexed with historical problems. By translating and transposing Shakespeare's *Othello* onto East Asia, the intercultural performance succeeds in recreating Shakespeare's play for contemporary local audiences. In considering this intercultural performance, this chapter explores the vital importance of local Shakespeare and local knowledge for the sake of global Shakespeare and its critical potential. An intercultural performance might evoke a divided response among a non-local audience. While on the one hand it attempts to create an "original" production of the Shakespeare play through the use of two Asian cultures, on the other it employs the Shakespeare play as a conduit for a cultural exchange between those two cultures; this is, and is not, Shakespeare. Finally, the chapter suggests that for all its ambivalence, the intercultural performance demonstrates some respectful if unfamiliar views that could be shared by many people around the globe.

Chapter 2 considers the Yamanote Jijosha theatre company's January 2015 production of *The Tempest*, directed by Masahiro Yasuda. At that time, Japan was still mourning the victims of the March 2011 earthquake and tsunami that devastated the Tohoku region and the meltdown of the Fukushima Daiichi nuclear power plant, unprecedented disasters that received exhaustive media coverage. In this context, this chapter critically explores the significance of performing Shakespeare in contemporary Japan as a version of intercultural exchange. The company's version of *The Tempest* reveals to contemporary Japanese audiences the ambiguity of Shakespeare's text by experimenting with the postdramatic and a new acting style. While critically pursuing the meaning and possibility of theatre and performing arts today, this staging of *The Tempest* powerfully presents a critical view of the blindness and superficiality of contemporary Japan and of the world represented in the play. Although Yasuda refers to Shakespeare's works as classics, this is not an old-fashioned play; rather, it is a deconstructed, glocalised (i.e., globally produced while simultaneously for a specific local audience) performance event revamped for its particular audience. We can reconfirm the value of extraordinary imagination on the verge of delusion and the creativity of theatre and performing arts through the company's intercultural and inventive adaptation of Shakespeare's work in Japan and abroad.

Chapter 3 deals with the last plays directed by Yukio Ninagawa (1935–2016), who had been expected to achieve the great milestone of directing the complete collection of Shakespeare plays in new Japanese translations before his death. This chapter reconsiders Ninagawa's direction from an intercultural–global–local perspective with a special focus on several of the last works he directed, namely *Richard II* (performed by young players of the Saitama Next Theatre in February 2012, which was especially intended for the Japanese audience), *NINAGAWA Macbeth* (performed in September 2015 and a revival of the director's internationally acclaimed production that was first performed in Japan in 1980 and abroad from 1985 onwards) and *Two Gentlemen of Verona* (the thirty-first in his series of Shakespeare plays and the seventh with an all-male cast, in October 2015). His last plays were not as brilliant as his earlier works because he was still experimenting with them. However, this chapter concludes that, when possessed by the power of theatre, Ninagawa's direction emitted its magical and subversive power and suggestion to give the audience the vital energy to live in this world of harsh conflict. He aimed to inspire wonder in the global and local spectators of the plays he directed.

Chapter 4 discusses the challenges and possibilities of multilingual performances of Shakespeare by examining a 2009 multilingual adaptation of *King Lear* directed by Tadashi Suzuki. This adaptation used four languages: German, English, Korean and Japanese. Translating and repositioning Shakespeare's *Lear* into the modern age, the adaptation succeeds in recreating Shakespeare's play for contemporary audiences. In considering the adaptation, this chapter explores the significance of multilingual performance in terms of Shakespeare's relevance in the twenty-first century. The adaptation could elicit a divided response from audience members who cannot understand all four languages. While on the one hand it attempts to create an "original" production of the Shakespeare play by using a mixture of Asian and European languages, on the other it exploits the Shakespeare play for multilingual theatrical experimentation and cultural exchange. The chapter concludes that, while the artistic value of this multilingual performance can certainly be appreciated, it anticipates the emergence of not a multilingual but a translingual performance of Shakespeare for the new age of communication and interconnectivity, whether digital or in person.

Chapter 5 discusses the study of translingual practice in worldwide Shakespeare performances, with a focus on *Henry V*. First, it surveys fundamental concepts and facts ranging from translingual practice, contact zones and contact languages through worldwide Shakespeare performances for foreigners in the age of global English and foreign languages in Shakespeare's works. The second part analyses two examples of translingual practice in the well-known wooing scene in *Henry V*, which has been called the most Babylonian of Shakespeare's plays. As the exchange between Katherine's (and Alice's) broken English and Henry's broken French shows, it ultimately does not matter whether their speeches are grammatically correct. What matters is the ability to interact with people of different linguistic and cultural backgrounds. This kind of translingual competence is universally required of humankind, no matter when the period is. More specifically, the two characters' translingual practice in the wooing scene represents linguistic and cultural contact and conflict. Although Henry's discourse is oppressive in this conquest play, the exchange is nevertheless highly significant: first, because it is an interesting example of the word "enemy" (*ennemi*) that can be both French and English, and second, because it uses mixed languages and semiotic resources and ecological affordances. The example of "enemy" is of particular interest since it reveals the instability of differences in languages, cultures and nationalities, along with their confusion and permeability. It suggests that the boundaries between self and other, languages, cultures and nationalities are not fixed but changeable and that many people live on the margins of these changing borders. The example reminds us that today we are expected to exist across or straddling borders and to interact with diverse people while retaining our own identities—which themselves are changeable—and integrating differences.

In an exploration of translingual performances of *King Lear*, Chapter 6 discusses *Lear Dreaming* (2012), directed by Ong Keng Sen, with a special focus on its environmental affordance and cognitive approach to scenography. The largely feminist version of *Lear* (1997) was adapted by Rio Kishida, a female Japanese playwright, and refashioned by Ong Keng Sen, a Singaporean director who is renowned for his intercultural productions. In 2012, Ong reconceived and directed *Lear* as the experimental *Lear Dreaming*. He reduced the number of players to four—two men and two women—and included a group of gamelan musicians (a traditional instrumental ensemble of Indonesia, typically including many bronze percussion instruments). In several scenes, the elder daughter (performed by a Chinese pipa—a shallow-bodied, four-stringed lute—player) expresses her mind through music with subtitles rather than through verbal exchanges. *Lear Dreaming* is distinguished by its effective use of music, laser beams and other scenic devices. As a rare example of a translingual adaptation of Shakespeare's play, it is thought-provoking, cutting-edge and appropriate for a new age.

Chapter 7 considers *Safaring the Night* (2017), an experimental production of *A Midsummer Night's Dream* adapted and directed by Yasuro Ito and set in virtual reality in 2045, the predicted year of so-called singularity. In this version, two artificial intelligence (AI) enterprises, Oberon and Titania, agree to be integrated, but it does not go well due to anti-AI terrorists who are actually humans. This chapter uses Ito's extremely complicated adaptation to explore several factors of semiotic resources, such as telepathic communication, projection mapping and the effect of a site-specific performance conducted in a mobile, interactive theatre, possibly the first experiment and certainly one of the first such experiments in the world. In this play, projection mapping is employed not simply for visual effect but as an essential part of the action. The audience members take part in the action, walk around the special venue and finally have to make a crucial decision. *Safaring the Night* is fantastic in the true sense of the word and especially relevant to a contemporary younger audience of digital/smartphone natives.

Part I

Intercultural and Multilingual Performance

Chapter 1

This Is, and Is Not, Shakespeare: A Japanese-Korean Transformation of *Othello*

Globalisation has led to localisation and identity politics. The linkage between the global and the local has, however, been ridden with contradictions because of cultural production that generates uneven cultural capital (Wilson and Dissanayake 5). If we hope to survive this late-capitalist system and postmodern ambivalence, we shall likely have to follow Zygmunt Bauman's suggestion (234-38) to aspire to transnational or cosmopolitan solidarity, as unfulfilled a dream as that might seem, while emphasising Shakespeare's hospitality towards strangers, as Richard Wilson (242-60) proposes.

The purpose of this chapter is to address the issue of global Shakespeare, chiefly by examining a Japanese-Korean intercultural performance of *Othello*. From the perspective of a reception specialist primarily interested in Shakespeare's current global status, this chapter also addresses the following issues: translation, adaptation, intercultural performance and the impact of the transformation of Shakespeare texts.

The question of global Shakespeare entails the question of local Shakespeare and, ultimately, the question of glocal Shakespeare. For centuries, Shakespeare's works have been read in English, translated into a vast number of languages and adapted and performed in a plethora of styles, local or otherwise. Through this process of global spread, Shakespeare has been naturalised, localised and even indigenised to such an extent that some non-English cultures regard him as a native author. No matter what we call this phenomenon—localisation, acculturation or cultural articulation—we find a collapse of the global and the local into the glocal.

The fundamental point of the apparently confusing tripartite question of global–local–glocal is that, whether or not our location is metropolitan, most of us are ambivalent about global Shakespeare. While we have great expectations for it, most of us have equally great anxiety about it. We tend to notice prominent postcolonial resistance against global Shakespeare or anger about uneven relations or exchange between metropolis and others and the West and the rest. Yet metropolitan academics themselves no longer seem to feel entirely secure. For example, the fourth British Shakespeare Association Conference was held in London in September 2009 under the theme "Local/Global Shakespeares." There, a leading British Shakespeare scholar, who co-authored *Shakespeare's Sonnets* (2004), declared, with tongue in cheek, that since the theme of the conference was local/global Shakespeare, he would like to present a local version, and read, with his co-author, sonnets in English with hilarious and incisive comments. We could easily note here both perennial British or metropolitan pride with a good sense of humour and sarcasm and counter-resistance against the force of putting any nation and culture (among others, English, the very nation and culture that produced the greatest poetic dramatist in the world) into a local status. In the British scholar's discourse, however, we can also find a symptom of the metropolitan anxiety about the uncertain consequences of the spread of global Shakespeare and about English cultural and linguistic identity, if not hegemony.

English Shakespeare today is now as much a global as a national phenomenon, and both his language and his thematic resources can be multiply exploited, at once from the inside—such as Shakespeare's plays in a Scottish accent and a number of popular or subcultural Shakespeare videos on YouTube as a kind of intracultural performance in the UK—and from the outside, as directors, performers and audiences triangulate among the local, global and personal landscapes of their worlds.[1]

Compared with the old global Shakespeare in previous centuries spread by British colonial rule and internationalism, Dionne and Kapadia (5) notice a new "global

Shakespeare" emerging in recent years—produced by the economic globalisation led by the United States, the rise of (American) English as a global language and new media technology—with critical reservations:

> There has been an explosion of critical interest in the way Shakespeare has been made to accommodate local cultures across the globe, a critical trend that works concurrently and in concert with the global English-speaking media aspiring to shape Shakespeare as an international artist. A new progressive internationalism has slowly and—some would say "at long last"—reshaped the academic discourses of intellectual labour in the profession of English in the United States, creating the opportunity for truly multiregional conferences and festivals to address a new "global Shakespeare."[2]

Resisting this new global Shakespeare and discourse, Dionne and Kapadia (7) focus on "the persistent indigenisation of Shakespeare" and intend to make Shakespeare "a site of contest." Suspicious of the global reach of the metropolitan knowledge of Shakespeare and texts at the expense of the ever-existing inequality between metropolitan discursive practice and its non-metropolitan counterpart, however, Orkin (2) writes:

> Without denying the simultaneous indispensability of the already existing shared achievements and knowledges of metropolitan Shakespeare scholarship, I want to argue that the kinds of knowledge that, especially, particularly non-metropolitan locations—whether they are located within twenty-first-century Europe and North America but outside the Shakespeare metropolitan academy, or beyond it—might afford, may themselves, in turn, offer additional opportunities for thinking about Shakespeare's plays.

In accord with his argument, this chapter contributes to reforming contemporary global Shakespeare through examining a local performance. It may be preferable to seek more positive glocalisation as an integration of globalisation and localisation than a collapse of the global and the local into the glocal as a phenomenon, beyond a fixed binary opposition between the global and the local. We could then appreciate glocal and intercultural performances of Shakespeare, whose power and knowledge are distributed with equity and shared by all local Shakespeares.

Reception and transformation specialists in non-English-speaking countries in particular are more acutely concerned with the impact of local Shakespeare on global Shakespeare. We try to explore its critical potential to interrogate contemporary global Shakespeare and accommodate a multiplicity of positions and diversity of voices towards the horizon of integrated glocal Shakespeare.

1. The Critical Impact of Local Shakespeare on Global Shakespeare: *Othello* in the Japanese *Mugen* Noh Style with Elements of Korean Shamanism: A Creative Subversion[3]

Shakespeare plays have been performed in Japan since the nineteenth century; more recently, it has been home to internationally well-known directors such as Tadashi Suzuki and Yukio Ninagawa. Korea was later to experience the plays, but their performances—and, in particular, their intercultural performances—are very popular today under distinguished directors such as Oh Tae-suk and Lee Youn-taek (Y. Lee 1-4).[4] Both countries have experienced intercultural performances from Shakespeare in a variety of styles—Western, traditional and experimental—and have enjoyed regular theatre exchanges since the early 1990s.

In 2005, Ku Na'uka performed *Othello in Noh Style*, an intercultural performance by Sukehiro Hirakawa of Shakespeare's *Othello* in Noh form. Lee Youn-taek, a leading Korean director who had been familiar with Miyagi's work for many years, was asked to direct *Othello in Noh Style* as a Japanese-Korean collaboration. This collaboration, performed in Seoul in 2008 and at Festival/Tokyo in 2009, was highly creative and transformative because of the synergy of the two experimental theatre companies and their styles. The performance incorporated elements of Korean shamanistic ritual and dance (*gut*) and elements from Japanese Noh to create a new reading of Shakespeare's *Othello*.

Before looking into the Japanese-Korean collaboration, it is crucial to discuss Ku Na'uka's *Othello in Noh Style*, which was directed by Miyagi. In Shakespeare's *Othello*, a Moor and Venetian lady fall in love despite differences in age and race. However, their love is the trigger that prompts a tragedy of jealousy and revenge. At Miyagi's request, Hirakawa adapted this tragedy replete with beauty and cruelty into a *mugen* (dream) Noh script. In his rewriting, the ghost of Desdemona, who was killed by Othello, lives on in the memory of her husband. *Othello in Noh Style* departs radically from the original tragedy, which follows Othello's descent into violent jealousy; instead, the Noh interpretation attempts to represent a world of *yūgen*—the Noh concept of profound and refined beauty that Zeami adapted from Japanese traditional aesthetics and made into a theatrical ideal. *Othello in Noh Style* is a story of the paradox of love and hatred between man and woman. The moment when Desdemona is murdered by her husband remains the most vital moment in her life; indeed, it is the moment that allows her ghost to continue to exist. Some might regard the pathos in this narrative thread as overwhelming, but this is precisely the central theme of the production. This rereading of *Othello* attempts to show that hope can emerge even within the Othello and Desdemona's broken marriage. Desdemona's passionate hope re-emerges despite everything, which prompts an emotionally moving reaction from the audience. In Miyagi's view, Noh has a function that modern theatre does not have; it is performed to relieve human loneliness. It presents the dynamic journey from the extreme of loneliness to the extreme of consolation.

Ku Na'uka's *Othello in Noh Style* is no longer a Western tragedy; it is transformed instead into a communal tragedy. Miyagi suggests that when Shakespeare's *Othello* is performed in Noh style, the darkness or hopelessness in the original is alleviated in some way. In the original play, it has long been recognised that it is extremely difficult to identify a sense of catharsis. *Othello in Noh Style* is the Japanese director's attempt to address this hopelessness by casting the tale in *mugen* Noh style, fusing Western and Eastern cultures and eventually providing a communal resolution to modern loneliness. This cultural fusion allows Shakespeare's play to be interpreted anew and admits the audience into the dimension of Desdemona's mind. Miyagi subverts Shakespeare's tragedy in a creative way, transforming it into a soul-consoling artistic work. Furthermore, Miyagi's reinterpretation or betrayal of the concept of Western tragedy is in fact creative, because it produces a highly original intercultural performance of a Shakespeare play with rich implications and spiritual depth.

In 2008, *Othello in Noh Style* was performed under Lee's direction with the collaboration of the leading members of Miyagi's company and two members of Lee's company. This production breathed new life into Shakespeare's *Othello*. Miyagi proposed the idea of *Othello* in *mugen* Noh style while exploring the strength of Japanese theatre. By using the Korean *gut* as a style with which to interpret *Othello*, Lee added elements of Korean shamanism to his interpretation and used a recognisable form of dialogue with a spirit, adopting the Korean ritualistic drama of *gut*. In his fused version, Lee used Noh to represent the world of deities and the dead; it is a dream or imaginary world. Korean shamanism then allowed a shaman to conduct dialogues with the dead, or rather with their spirits. By combining Noh and *gut* in his production, Lee hoped that the idealistic elements of both the Japanese and Korean cultures could form a fused, ideal world in *Othello*.

While directing *Othello in Noh Style* for the new collaborative Japanese-Korean production, Lee noticed the common threads that ran through both *gut* and the *mugen* Noh style and tried to fuse these traditions through classic English drama. Scenes from Shakespeare's original play are performed in the two interludes, but the locations for the main events of the Japanese-Korean collaboration are transferred from Venice to the Korean Peninsula and from Cyprus to Okinawa, while the style shifts between *mugen* Noh and *gut*.

The Japanese-Korean version of *Othello* is set two thousand years ago and located on an island in ancient Asia, where a sad and cruel story of love between a woman of the Korean Peninsula and a man of Okinawa is developed. Desdemona is a person from Korea, and Othello is a dark southerner and man of the sea from Okinawa; East Asia becomes the location of the action instead of the Mediterranean Sea in Shakespeare's original. The Japanese-Korean collaboration superimposes the ancient history of East Asia onto the story of early modern Europe; in this version, the tale is more multi-layered and complex, and these changes can expand the play on an epic scale by increasing the cultural complexity and dynamism and widening the focus. Furthermore, Lee adopts a directional strategy that does not aim to emulate Western text-based realism; instead, he employs an Asian style, focusing on visuality, physicality and musicality.

The ending of Lee's *Othello* differs both from Shakespeare's original play and from Miyagi's *mugen* Noh version in that it involves a Korean theatrical parade with musicians coming onto the stage immediately before the play ends. In fact, Othello and Desdemona appear hand in hand, walking alongside other characters! In addition, the violent ending of Shakespeare's tragedy is modified in both versions. In the *mugen* Noh version, the gruesome conclusion is displaced by a quiet and peaceful ending, while the *gut* version transformed it into a festive comedy. Both Asian versions modify the darkness of the original ending into a lighter finale. The lively ending of Lee's version is unimaginable in both Shakespeare's tragedy and the Noh play. In the latter, all the actors, musicians and singers exit in silence, leaving the stage empty in an effort to allow the audience to empty and purify their own minds.

In discussing the difference between the *mugen* Noh version and the *gut* version, Lee suggests that, ideally, no tragedy should exist in Korea, since pain and grief are released communally by spirits and living people in Korean culture (Post-performance talk). At the end of *Othello in Noh Style*, the audience feels a sense of catharsis or purification, while as Lee's *Othello* comes to a close, the audience is distracted from the horrible tragedy and soon engrossed in the sense of play that infuses the next scene, which focuses on the shamanistic and festive atmosphere of song and dance. Miyagi felt that a Japanese audience would not feel purified by watching Shakespeare's *Othello* in its original form, and he asked Hirakawa to adapt it into a Noh version. As has previously been made clear, the Noh version transformed the Western tragedy into a hybrid play with both Western and Eastern elements.

For Lee, the priority in creating an intercultural performance is to encourage exchange and negotiations among Asian theatres; with this in mind, it seems likely that he is attempting to betray the very concept of Western tragedy. Lee's *Othello* does significantly transform Shakespeare's tragedy; nonetheless, the transformation is a theatrical pleasure for most local audiences. The Korean director committed a creative subversion of Miyagi's expectations by boldly creating a play that went beyond those expectations. Shakespeare's tragedy is transplanted into another culture in ancient East Asia, and the tragedy becomes transformed through Noh and *gut* into an alternative theatrical experience in which the audience finds a sense of relief and joy.

Shakespeare's great tragedies, including *Othello,* do address fundamental problems of human existence such as evil, death and suffering. Unlike other familiar tragic productions that end with the catastrophic death of the main characters on the stage, this intercultural production of *Othello* goes further. Rather than limiting itself to only representing death and suffering, the Japanese-Korean intercultural performance of *Othello* also explores notions of consolation. Inspired by both the *mugen* Noh tendency to see the world from the perspective of the dead and the Korean shamanism that connects this world with the other world, the intercultural performance extends the notions of grief and suffering to include explorations of release. This suggests that this new reading of *Othello* is a creative subversion.

2. The Critical Impact of the Japanese-Korean Adaptation of *Othello* on Global Shakespeare

2.1. Translation Matters

Sukehiro Hirakawa, a polyglot and a distinguished Japanese scholar of comparative literature, adapted Shakespeare's *Othello* into a Noh script. When he directed it, Miyagi added several interludes in which scenes from the original text were performed. Miyagi used a Japanese translation by Yūshi Odashima, whose translations of the complete works of Shakespeare were published between 1973 and 1980. Odashima's translation style is famous for wordplay and speed and for making Shakespeare's plays seem as if they are contemporary plays in Japanese. Both *Othello in Noh Style* and the Japanese-Korean collaboration are, however, characterised more by their intercultural performances than by their translations. This section, therefore, confirms several matters of translation as a prerequisite to intercultural performance.

First, responding to Walter Benjamin's famous essay "The Task of the Translator," Derrida, who had a lifelong interest in the question of translation, writes about the primal importance of translation:

> Nothing is more serious than a translation. I rather wished to mark the fact that every translator is in a position to speak *about* translation, in a place that is

certainly not second or secondary. For if the structure of the original is marked by the requirement to be translated, it is because in laying down the law, the original begins by indebting itself *as well* with regard to the translator. The original is the first debtor, the first petitioner; it begins by lacking—and by pleading for translation. (207)

Derrida adds:

If the translator neither restitutes nor copies an original, it is because the original lives on and transforms itself. In truth, the translation will be a moment in the growth of the original, which will complete itself in enlarging itself. (211)

Although he does not say that any translation will do, Derrida's thoughts are deeply insightful in relation to the position that the original demands translation because of its primary lack and that the translation will complement it and contribute to its growth. This complementary or symbiotic relationship between the original and the translation is suggestive in reconsidering local and global Shakespeare; it is almost certainly the case that global Shakespeare demands local Shakespeare.

There have recently been important developments in Shakespeare translation studies. In *Shakespeare and the Language of Translation*, among other works, the editor Ton Hoenselaars (1-27) seeks to demonstrate that meaning is not permanently rooted in the original text of Shakespeare but is to a large extent determined by the context; thus, we come to realise that every new translation makes Shakespeare "more contemporary." This means not only that translation makes Shakespeare's early modern English more accessible in each location but also that by making Shakespeare more contemporary, translation makes Shakespeare more meaningful and interesting for today's audience and reader. Most of Shakespeare's plays were already familiar to the initial audiences in Elizabethan and early Jacobean London. It is quite sensible to attempt to make Shakespeare's texts more contemporary today in order to reconstruct the initial relationship between text and audience. We may be able to obtain glimpses into the original theatrical space of the Globe through the "contemporary" effect produced by translation.

2.2. Intercultural Performance Matters

Since the Japanese-Korean *Othello* collaboration is an intercultural performance, both interculturalism and intercultural performance are discussed here. Interculturalism is a controversial topic in theatre studies since it presents theoretical and practical difficulties, problems and even dangers that range from excessive desire for others to the increasing complexity of contemporary cultural exchange, transformation and hybridisation. Interculturalism itself derives from Orientalism, which still overshadows its development. Interculturalism has been described as:

> A means of imagining culture as a landscape which, when occupied, produces, transmits, and substitutes for a once authentic culture. Rather than a mutual meeting in a space between cultures, intercultural performance is most often a practice of the desire, imagination and anxieties of the one cultural system that looks to the other culture for formalist or aesthetic templates for the renovation of itself. Intercultural theatre thus operates in the space between two or more cultures, but those cultures themselves rarely, if ever, meet, let alone interact. (Singleton, "Interculuralism" 630; see also Bennett 166-203, Bharucha 3-6, Hodgdon 158-59, Shepherd and Wallis 198-206, Yong, "Shakespeare and the Fiction of the Intercultural" 527-49, Zarrilli 108-133.)

In discussing Shakespearean geographies, Worthen (*Shakespeare and the Force* 130) writes that "European intercultural performance is firmly conjoined to the history of imperial expansion," and further that "the globalized economy is the condition of intercultural performance today." "A new form of interculturalism" (Singleton 195) is, therefore, expected to replace the existing version, Western or otherwise.[5]

In *Intercultural Performance and Appropriation*, Sanders (9) writes:

> Intercultural performance could be defined as an inherently conservative genre…. Yet, as the notion of hostile takeover present in a term such as "appropriation" implies, intercultural performance can also be oppositional, even subversive. There are as many opportunities for divergence as adherence, for assault as well as homage.

In relation to the present chapter, it is of great interest that Sanders (20) also notes that "it is usually at the very point of infidelity that the most creative acts of intercultural performance and appropriation take place."

In this intercultural performance, Japanese and Korean theatre powerfully interact with each other. Local Shakespeare functions as a cultural catalyst for two nations that have been vexed with historical problems but runs the risk of being appropriated by the global Shakespeare industry. Translating and repositioning Shakespeare's *Othello* into East Asia, adapting and subverting the Orientalism that is inherent in the original text, the Japanese Korean intercultural performance of Othello succeeds in recreating Shakespeare's play for contemporary and local audiences.

Miyagi believes that those involved in theatre must deal both with Western drama—classical and modern—and Japanese classical drama. He is also very concerned with "the pan-East-Asian" identity in all its manifestations, an identity that he regards as in constant flux. Through performing in India, Korea, China and Tibet, Miyagi has become aware of the perennial interactions that have occurred among

Asian cultures and the exchanges that inform the various senses of beauty throughout the region. For this reason, he now finds it meaningless to differentiate between an original theatre work and a so-called copy in Asia, despite the fact that there appear to be significant differences between types of regional theatre. Miyagi prioritises cultural commensurability in all his work, especially what he sees as a pan-East-Asian commonality and a common Asian cultural connection, pursuing an intercultural or transcultural performance. In the current critical and theoretical climate, however, this notion of a common cross-cultural theatrical form might be criticised for homogenising diverse cultural and theatrical forms and traditions by assimilating them all into a single pan-East-Asian framework.

While a plethora of Shakespeare productions, theatre histories and forms have been produced around the world, the research conducted on them has been extremely fragmented, even disjointed. The lack of a unified overview of the global interpretations of Shakespeare reflects, in part, their dazzling complexity and dynamism. Confronted with the ever-increasing linguistic, cultural and interpretative diversity of Shakespearean productions, most Shakespeare scholars in this age of cultural pluralism and postcolonialism are careful to avow that diversity. However, no holistic paradigm of intercultural Shakespeare productions has yet been established. If we keep in mind the cultural value differences that exist among diverse cultures without essentialising them, then it is clear that Miyagi's general view may well be significant in attempting to outline this holistic paradigm, which would be of great significance.

By combining Noh style with *gut* in his production, Lee hopes that the idealistic elements of both the Japanese and Korean cultures can form a fused, ideal world in *Othello*. However, Lee was aware of the potential perils of this method. Any production that combined Shakespeare's original play with both Japan's Noh and Korea's shamanism could easily become mere spectacle. Despite this danger, he regarded the project as worthwhile and rewarding. Lee believed that this fusion of styles was valid, since "Western theatre originates in the Dionysian festival" (Interview, my translation); this is similar to Japanese and Korean theatre, both of which originate in ritualistic festivals. Lee concludes his interview as follows:

> After all, the world is one. I believe that all people have the same feeling about rituals. Whether Shakespearean drama, Japanese tradition, *gut* or shamanism, they all originate at the same source, and therefore, there must be a way for them to communicate with each other. The task of finding this way will be difficult, but I think it will be fun.

Festival/Tokyo is held not only to showcase conventional and popular works as a form of cultural tourism but also to expose people to works with which they may be unfamiliar but that demonstrate new artistic expressions and values. The members of the festival's executive committee are keen to ensure that the festival remains avant-garde and provocative, challenging the local and global artistic mainstream. Against this wider framework of the festival, it is clear that Lee's firm belief in international cultural exchange reflects the values of the festival well and offers a significant challenge to the contemporary theatre scene. More important, his belief and practice contribute to reforming global Shakespeare.

The Japanese-Korean intercultural performance of *Othello* has several features as described in section 2.1, of which the most striking is its great concern with Desdemona's soul. In the Japanese Noh version, the main focus is on her salvation, as it is in the Japanese-Korean intercultural performance. Shakespeare's text is open to a variety of readings, as it contains a medley of Christian and non-Christian ideas about life and death. Having said this, Shakespeare criticism is mainly concerned with the racial issue of Othello as a stranger. It is uncertain why the majority of audiences and theatre people seem to care so little about Desdemona's post-mortem well-being. It might be attributed to Othello's speech suggesting, in his mind, her salvation: "When we shall meet at compt / This look of thine will hurl my soul from heaven / And fiends will snatch at it" (5.2.271-73).[6]

Among the many intercultural performances of *Othello*, the feminist intercultural performance or rather appropriation is the most remarkable since the late twentieth century (e.g., Paula Vogel's *Desdemona: A Play about a Handkerchief* (1993)). Vogel transforms Shakespeare's heroine into a sexually liberated woman; she could be said to have "saved" Desdemona from the status of a passive victim by endowing her with agency. Yet Vogel has no concern with Desdemona's spiritual condition after her death. The same is true of Ann-Marie MacDonald's *Goodnight Desdemona (Good Morning Juliet)* (1988) and Toni Morrison's *Desdemona* (2011).

It is thus almost certainly correct to say that the Japanese-Korean intercultural performance's concern with Desdemona's salvation is unique. As some members of the Japanese audience felt uncomfortable with Lee's festive ending, clearly not everybody can or will appreciate it, perhaps finding it to be a transgression of the original. Whether or not audiences or readers can appreciate it, it is evident that the most creative act of intercultural performance takes place at the very point of infidelity.

In fact, the Japanese-Korean intercultural performance sheds light on Shakespeare's unique culture. In the Christian tradition, each individual's salvation or damnation will be finally determined by God. In Japanese and Korean traditions (influenced by Buddhism, Taoism, Shinto and shamanism), what matters most is not each individual's salvation but collective salvation through a communal ritual. This local Shakespeare has a critical impact on global Shakespeare through its cross-cultural questioning, reception and transformation, or creative subversion. The ending of the Japanese-Korean intercultural performance is thought-provoking, since the uniqueness of Shakespeare's original text—its cultural context as well as its Christian background—is disclosed, questioned and subverted.

In considering the Japanese-Korean intercultural performance of *Othello*, this chapter has explored the vital importance of local Shakespeare and local knowledge for the sake of global Shakespeare as critical potential. The intercultural performance might evoke a divided response among a non-local audience. While it attempts to create an "original" production of the Shakespeare play by using two Asian cultures, it also employs the Shakespeare play as a conduit for their cultural exchange. This is, and is not, Shakespeare. However, what we have here is not ambivalence. The intercultural performance reveals respectful, if unfamiliar, feelings that could be shared by many people around the globe.

There remain, however, Derridaesque questions: is it possible to gather under a single roof the apparently disordered plurivocity of the world's Shakespeare reproductions? Is it possible to find a rule of cohabitation, it being understood that this house will always be haunted by the meaning of the original? Nobody can give a final answer to these interrelated questions with confidence; nevertheless, despite many possible difficulties and challenges, we should certainly aim for the goal of a new global Shakespeare with a spirit of developing intense cultural sensitivity.

Chapter 2

Performing Shakespeare after the 11 March 2011 Disaster: Yamanote Jijosha's *The Tempest*

Valuable books and papers on Shakespeare in modern Japan and Asia have been published (Kawachi; Kennedy and Yong; Kishi and Bradshaw; Minami et al.; Sasayama et al.; Trivedi and Miami); therefore, this chapter does not discuss attempts in Japanese and other Asian theatres to adapt, appropriate or acculturate Shakespeare to their respective times and locations. Instead, it focuses on their early imitation and later radical criticism of (possibly anachronistic) Western realist productions of Shakespeare's plays, which were originally written and performed in early modern England. This chapter considers as case material the Yamanote Jijosha theatre company's *The Tempest* performed at Theatre East, Tokyo Metropolitan Theatre in January 2015. At that time, Japan was still mourning the victims—18,475 dead and missing —of the 11 March 2011 earthquake and tsunami in the Tohoku region and the meltdown of the Fukushima Daiichi nuclear power plant, unprecedented disasters which the media covered extensively. With this background, the chapter critically explores the significance of performing Shakespeare in contemporary Japan.

Numerous Japanese theatre companies, mainstream and otherwise, have frequently performed Shakespeare's plays. Among these, Yamanote Jijosha, a small company based in central Tokyo, merits special consideration as it has experimented with performing Shakespearean plays (*A Midsummer Night's Dream, Macbeth, Titus Andronicus, Romeo and Juliet* and *Troilus and Cressida*) in a variety of ways since 1995, partly inspired by Polish avant-garde theatrical theory and practice. In 2006, the company invited Piotr Cieslak, art director of Theatre Dramatyczny Warsaw in Poland, and actress Julia Kijowska to produce *Ivona, Princess of Burgundia*, written for the theatre company in 1938 by the famous Polish émigré novelist and playwright Witold Gombrowicz (1904–1969) (Yamanote Jijosha). Interest in Gombrowicz's plays, which anticipated the theatre of the absurd, revived in the 1960s (Krzyzanowski). In particular, Yamanote Jijosha, while performing in Eastern European countries including Poland, developed a special relationship with Polish theatre, from Yasuda's continuing interest in Jerzy Grotowski's acting training and theatrical experiments to his appreciation of Jan Kott's *Shakespeare Our Contemporary* (first published in English in 1964 and translated into Japanese in 1968).

Masahiro Yasuda and fellow Waseda University students founded Yamanote Jijosha in Tokyo:

> Since its foundation, the company has sought to create an acting style that expresses the way of living of contemporary Japanese through group creation. One of its early experiments was called "hyper-collage," simultaneous enacting of different stories on the stage. Now it is well-known for its unique performance style (known as "yojohan") and highly evaluated original reinterpretations of the classic texts of Japan as well as the West. (Yasuda, *Yamanote Jijosha 1984* 2)

In addition, the company is acclaimed for its original reinterpretations of classic Japanese and Western texts. Its recent productions include a retelling of a famous Noh play *Dojyoji* (2004 based on three different sources of the same name and performed in Japan and later abroad), *Titus Andronicus* (performed at the 2009 Sibiu International Festival in Romania) and *Hedda Gabler* (2014).

Discussing the company's *Titus Andronicus*, Mika Eglinton points out that Yasuda's trip to a 1997 theatre festival in Avignon in search of an alternative style of acting not only led him "to explore territory outside the confines of Western realism, but it also prompted the director to question his cultural identity as a Japanese theatre practitioner" ("Performing Constraint" 16). Yasuda subsequently developed the *yojohan* acting method. Deeming so-called Western realist acting insufficient to reflect the realities of life in contemporary Japan, he hoped to radically deconstruct "the conditions that characterised the acting styles of Japanese traditional theatre" and confine "the movements of actors to the space of a typical Japanese tearoom size, yojohan" (Yasuda, "*Yojohan*"). Yasuda believed that *yojohan* physically defines the movements of Japanese people, symbolises the sense of constraint that many Japanese feel when caught between duty and desire and relates to the state of high mental concentration required of participants in tea ceremonies. Based on this theory, Yasuda lays out rules that actors should observe as they perform:

> While standing still, pull away from the centre of gravity in your body; while moving, imagine as if you were going along a narrow path; when spoken to by another actor, freeze on the spot and listen to his/her lines attentively; when no one speaks to you, continue your movement in a slow motion. By imposing these restrictions on the movements of actors, they can express how modern Japanese people sensitively and even neurotically react to their surroundings and other people. (Yasuda, "*Yojohan*")

Yasuda's company might seem to employ an extremely localised and constrained acting style called *kata*. This style clearly is rooted in a contemporary urban Japanese sense of life, but its sense of concentration and restraint is felt by many people living in today's cities throughout the world. This style originated from physical acts commonly performed by Japanese people conditioned by high population density and narrow spaces. It produces highly dramatic energy which appeals to audience members, awakening them to strange, beautiful impulses and drives hidden in their bodies. Yasuda's concept of *kata* "goes against the term's traditional meaning, which is a set of predetermined, refined, and imparted to an apprentice by a master, as in the case of *kabuki* actor training"; instead, *kata* is "constantly subject to revision as social structures and expressions of cultures evolve" (Eglinton, "Performing Constraint" 18). *Yojohan*, therefore, is both local and global, both strict and flexible.

In addition to *yojohan*, Yamanote Jijosha has developed the Yamanote method of training actors, which includes body exercise through free improvisation and RPAM, which is the "the combination of rhythm, play, acting and movement [and] a kind of dance specially designed for modern Japanese actors who lack movement literacy such as ballet and Japanese dancing" (Yasuda, *Yamanote Jijosha 1984* 18). In *The Tempest*, the company's actors performed sophisticated versions of RPAM, which they choreographed themselves and entitled "the tempest," "the island," "nostalgia" and "illusion." When successful, Yamanote Jijosha's unique method and underlying philosophy create magic in theatre, or an "efficient and intangible vital force" that is "to some extent similar to what is referred to with the magical nature of Mana, which specialists in the field defines as the energetic of immaterial substance of a human body or object (Maniutiu 244-45).

As suggested by the company's engagement in improvisation and RPAM, its director Yasuda is aware of the postdramatic shift from work to event, or from text-based performance to performance event, in contemporary theatre and the performing arts, including Shakespeare performance and studies (Worthen, *Shakespeare Performance Studies* 3-29). His company has experimented with the intensely dramatic and the postdramatic while attempting to emancipate generally passive spectators and make them participants.

Reviewing Yamanote Jijosha's *The Tempest*, Tetsuya Motohashi, a postcolonialist Japanese theatre critic, argues that its presentation of the violence of representation inflicted by the West on natives stems from the director's understanding of postcolonial criticism. Although Motohashi does not mention the Japanese elements of the play in his review, the company performs *The Tempest* not only as a postcolonialist work but also as a play to which contemporary Japanese audiences can relate, as discussed in this chapter, particularly section 3.

1. *The Tempest* as Prospero's Apocalyptic Delusion

Following his usual practice, Yasuda composed a script for his company's performance of *The Tempest* using modern Japanese translations by Yūshi Odashima, Kazuko Matsuoka and Minoru Toyota. When effective for his purposes, he also cites or mixes lines from Shakespeare's other plays and other playwrights' works. In *Titus Andronicus*, he conflates Shakespeare's play and Heiner Müller's *Anatomie of Titus: Fall of Rome Ein Shakespearekommentar*, rearranged by Yasuda and translated by Eglinton ("Performing Constraint" 24). In *The Tempest*, Yasuda quotes famous lines from *Hamlet* and adds a traditional Japanese folk song and a popular song, making the performance hybrid and multicultural. Shakespeare's text is deconstructed, and the company presents drastically grotesque—at times obscene and comic—physicality and theatricality to picture the world as driven by sexual desire, political power struggles and violence among Prospero, Miranda and Caliban, Prospero, Miranda and Ferdinand, Caliban, Trinculo and Stephano and Jovanna (Queen of Naples), Sebastian and Antonio.

In the director's note to the "Programme of *The Tempest*," Yasuda writes that the play is often said to be about "pardoning humans"; however, when so read, it becomes boring. Therefore, his company presents the play as demonstrating that "humans are not pardoned." The play shows Prospero's growing awareness that he himself cannot be pardoned. All the persons of whom Prospero has taken care—Miranda, Ariel and

Caliban—betray him, letting him see his true self. He finds in Caliban the detestable aspect of himself that he has repressed, in Ariel the disorder of his own delusion and in Miranda the vulgarity of his own blood. The tempest in this play is neither in the sea nor on the island but in Prospero's own mind.

The man who cannot forgive himself also can and cannot forgive others; rather, from the start, it is clear that he will forgive the Queen (not the King in this production) of Naples before he creates the tempest. Yasuda ("Programme") writes that his company hopes to perform the sight that the self-unforgiven man comes to see. This bitter, distressing condition is the *mise-en-scène* of Yamanote Jijosha's bold reinterpretation of *The Tempest*.

Miranda, in particular, is reinterpreted in this production. She does not look like Prospero's daughter but is middle-aged and resembles his wife or a prostitute. Although realistically she could not have grown to middle age in the twelve years since she and her father were exiled from Milan when she was an infant, this production liberates itself from the fixed, boring image of a pretty, chaste girl; she has her own desire and expresses it aggressively. Whether for good or ill, the spectators see a completely new image of Miranda; she is sensuous, clever and at times comic, in full possession of her agency. Disdaining Caliban's lust for her, she sometimes enjoys comically having incestuous intercourse with her father on stage. When later courted by Ferdinand, she treats him sadistically.

Prospero fears that he cannot be pardoned because of his past crimes and his persistent dark desire. His painful memory and hopeless vision of the future afflict him. Despite his great sense of crimes and despair, he is far from a Renaissance magus; rather, he has become transformed into an ordinary street magician or quack. His contradictions and limitations aggravate his distress.

The play-within-a-play scene (masque) in Act 5 reveals Prospero's limitations and contradictions. This scene, performed by fairies, is radically deconstructed and enacted as Prospero's nightmare. In the middle of the masque, the lights grow darker, and he falls into a nightmare that exposes his fear and obsession. In that nightmare, he is killed by Caliban, Trinculo and Stephano and put into a coffin filled with books. Prospero then throws away the books and, quoting Hamlet's suicidal soliloquy, says with a frown:

> To be, or not to be, that is the question....
> To die, to sleep—
> No more....
> To die, to sleep—
> To sleep—perchance to dream: ay, there's the rub
> For in that sleep of death what dreams may come.... (3.1.56-66)

Prospero's dream in this production represents his own death as a loss of his desire. He is revenged on himself by his own delusion. The Yamanote Jijosha's *yojohan* method yields effective performances of the breath-taking murder and resurrection of Prospero in particular.

In a critical close reading of *The Tempest*, Yasuda came to doubt its prevailing vague and romantic interpretation and to feel that, instead, it presents Shakespeare's prophesy of the coming apocalypse of humankind (personal communication, 18 Dec. 2014). Although Prospero in this production is driven to lord over his slaves, his subordinates subvert and betray him until he comes to say, "This thing of darkness I / Acknowledge mine" (5.1.275-76). Prospero acknowledges the darker side of humanity and Caliban's lust for Miranda as his own.

In contrast with the master-slave relationship of Prospero and Caliban characterised by mutual hatred and dependency, the spirit Ariel performs and signifies something special and elusive, although "it," like Caliban, is under Prospero's control.

Today, Ariel is played by male and female actors, and the representation and gender issues of this character have been widely discussed:

> But Ariel is a spirit, as he later reminds Prospero, without human feeling (5.1.20) — and the variety of disguises the spirit assumes throughout the play suggests a protean being without a fixed human shape.... Shakespeare's treatment of Ariel seems designed to remove the spirit from the human world, to make the character a sexless shape-shifter, an "it" rather than a "she" or "he." (Dymkowski 34-35)

Discussing the question of Ariel's indeterminacy in terms of transversal poetics, Reynolds and Thompson contend that "by embracing Ariel's textually determined feature, its otherworldliness, the character retains its transversally empowering ambiguity, even if played within the confines of the human form" (207). They propose several non-human representations of Ariel, such as "a metal-based robot" and "a non-gendered nude" (Reynolds and Thompson 207):

> These means of dehumanizing Shakespeare's sprite would free Ariel from the bounds of meaning socially prescribed onto it, as well as onto audiences, and would allow Ariel's inspriteful indeterminacy to be harnessed in order to inspire transversal tempests both off and on the stage. (Reynolds and Thompson 208)

In Yamanote Jijosha's *The Tempest*, Koki Ura, one of the company's most skilled actors in *yojohan*, plays Ariel as sexless and genderless, often with a mischievous smile, wearing small flowers and weeds in its hair, sporting a partially painted face and patchy costume and always barefoot. While executing Prospero's orders, Ariel appears suddenly and enjoys watching the confusion that causes among other characters.

The spirit also connects the stage with the auditorium, for example by sitting in the aisle and using a loudspeaker to agitate the other characters in the spirit of fun. Ura performs Ariel as an acrobatic magician who becomes a menace to his master Prospero, who is plagued by internal conflicts. The non-human Ariel is free from crimes, memory, dark desire and any other human element, from past illusion, present pain and any ideology or faith; consequently, he can inflict violence on humans and think it fun. In the end, Ariel is liberated from Prospero's power. This spirit which signifies transversal power might suggest the only hope for a better future for humans. Ariel has left before Prospero's epilogue ends the play, aligning this approach with Shakespeare's text. The spirit is an emancipated being, free of the order of the world: a state to which most humans aspire.

Though Prospero is destined to pardon the crimes committed by his deceivers (his brother, the Queen of Naples and Caliban), he does not feel himself pardoned from his crimes at the end of the tempest brought about by his rough magic (or a delusion in his mind). The word "despair" in his epilogue thus takes on special emphasis:

> Now my charms are all o'erthrown,
> And what strength I have's mine own,
> Which is most faint...
> Now I want
> Spirits to enforce, art to enchant;
> And my ending is *despair*,
> Unless I be relieved by prayer,
> Which pierce so that it assaults
> Mercy itself, and frees all faults.
> As you from crimes would pardoned be,
> Let your indulgence set me free. (Epilogue 1-20; italics added)

The world falls apart, leaving behind signs in leaves and broken objects. Yasuda's direction, which incorporates elements like a wonder cabinet, shows the influence of strong images from the postmodern film *Prospero's Books* (1991), written and directed by Peter Greenaway. Prospero, stricken with conflicts, pain, anxiety and horror, on the border between sanity and insanity, delusion and reality, a being materially and mentally falling in a destroyed world, is lit and lifted in the air by spirits for a moment, after which the stage is plunged into darkness. His emphatic statement of "despair" rings in the audience's ears. As Prospero's play ends, the audience must depart for a future that, in all probability, will not be easy. Amid the diversity of sounds created by the spirits, some of which might sound heavenly, the apocalyptic and catastrophic sound effects and clashing noises and visual effects used by Yamanote Jijosha throughout its performance of *The Tempest* reminded the Japanese audience of the contemporary counterpart: the natural and technological disasters in the Tohoku district and the Fukushima Daiichi nuclear power plant on 11 March 2011.

2. Caliban's Binding and Torture on Stage

In the first scene showing the tempest caused by Prospero's magic on the dark stage, sailors and other characters do not speak, while spirits portray the violent tempest through gestures and physical movements, tearing the sailors' clothes. Using letters, pictures and signs drawn on boards and pieces of paper, the spirits depict the sea and the shipwreck. Spectators might see this stage structure as a mirror or parallel world. The performance event on the stage could be Prospero's illusion; the exiled duke of Milan has sought revenge and, in a delusion, Prospero imagines that the Queen of Naples, his wicked brother Antonio and their party are at last sailing to his island.

One of the greatest inventions in Yamanote Jijosha's *The Tempest* is the presentation of another secondary or imaginary Caliban, bound and sometimes tortured in the bottom of a slave ship throughout almost the entire performance event as it unfolds on centre stage. As if in the mirror world, a naked figure is bound at stage right and at times is afflicted with convulsions, groans or cries in pain. Yasuda is keenly aware of colonial violence as he deploys triple Calibans on stage: Caliban proper, an icon of Western colonialism, along with his two illusions. The bound, tortured Caliban in a slave ship writhes in pain; when he groans, the ship lists and the chandeliers shake. Colonial violence on the slave's body is powerfully represented in the blinking lights and the squeaking sound of the bed. In this production, looking at this tortured self, the genuine Caliban says, "He is myself. That's my identity" (Motohashi). The bound Caliban is the genuine Caliban's self in his memory as a slave, which he can now recognise. Another Caliban appears as a slave-driver who tortures the slave as a coloniser's instrument. The layered representation of Caliban as native, slave and slave-driver is profoundly insightful (Motohashi).

More disturbingly, the presence of the illusory Caliban bound and tortured on the stage makes the spectators witness not only past colonial violence but the dark, cruel realities of the world then and now. His pain and groans do not allow the audience members to remain passive spectators but make them perceive their own ethical responsibilities and their participation in history.

3. An Additional Japanese Ending

In the director's note about *The Tempest*, Yasuda states that he always attempts to include contemporary Japan on the stage. He thinks that Prospero's farewell to Ariel and throwing away of his magic—his delusion—represent the problematic condition of contemporary Japan, where most detest the dubiousness of delusion but ironically have difficulty finding hope or vision (Yasuda, "Programme"). Prospero, who is an ordinary street magician throughout most of the play, comes to represent contemporary Japanese at its conclusion.

The company's ending to *The Tempest* appears moderate, with the great exception of Prospero's apparent sudden death before his return voyage, compared to these other radical endings. For instance, in the ending of Yamanote Jijosha's *Titus Andronicus*, performed in the shadow of the 9/11 attacks, the revenge cycle ends with the death of Titus, but another cycle is born with the rise of Aaron as a terrorist, who alone rises and walks menacingly along an imagined, narrow path into our daily world (Yasuda, "Talk" 4). In a 2009 postcolonialist production of *The Tempest* directed by Janice Honeyman, as "Prospero leaves the stage, Caliban, throwing off the two crutches he has been leaning on all through the performance, is the last visual image before the lights black out" (Heijes 139). Similarly, Yamanote Jijosha's *The Tempest*, radically and critically questions the contemporary Japanese way of life represented by Prospero. Life itself appears as a kind of magic containing all elements, from the grotesque and dubious to the erotic and violent to the beautiful. In the pursuit of the cool, comfortable, easy and rational, contemporary Japanese do not face the reality or truth of life. In Yasuda's view, those who cannot look at reality, regardless of how grotesque or hopeless it might be, cannot find true hope or vision, as those who have experienced the bottom of life dare to seek. The ending of Yamanote Jijosha's *The Tempest* presents a powerful, critical view of the blindness and superficiality of contemporary Japanese society.

When the epilogue is spoken, the stage goes black save for a spotlight left on the grief-stricken Prospero lifted at centre, as discussed in section 1. His emphatically spoken "despair" hangs in the air as the audience listens in darkness to legendary popular singer Momoe Yamaguchi's song "Iihi Tabidachi" ("Days That Used to Be").[1] Following the company's practice of using a mix of Western, Asian, classical and popular music, *The Tempest* presents, among others, Western classics and traditional

Japanese folk songs and instruments like pipes. The play concludes with Yamaguchi's song:

> I hear a voice—It sings to me
> The ancient calling of the sea
> It's bringing back to me a memory
> Of days that used to be
> My dear old friends—I remember them
> They'll never pass this way again
> I'm left alone, and I think back then
> Of days that used to be
> Somewhere someone is waiting just for me
> A special someone who shares the calling, calling of the sea ...
> I'm gonna leave the past behind
> And shake all sad thoughts out of my mind
> I know a new life now I will find
> But what must be, will be.[2]

Yasuda makes the audience listen to this sentimental, well-known J-Pop song for several possible reasons. Except for the reference to the sea, there is no overt connection between Shakespeare's play and the song, the original version of which suggests the northern Japan Sea. As Prospero seems ready to return to his homeland, the narrator of in this song prepares to depart on a journey, likely to the north. Life is not always easy; indeed, it seems to be becoming harder in contemporary Japan. The song, with which most Japanese are familiar, serves as a device to bring the Japanese audience members from the violent performance event on stage back to their daily lives with a sense of familiarity, sentimentality and consolation. At the same time, the song recalls for the audience the

11 March apocalyptic disaster in the Tohoku region. Reflecting contemporary Japan and taking a critical view of the nation, the song helps the Japanese audience feel relief while mourning the victims of the great disaster.

Shakespeare has long been respected as a great British dramatist and has been translated, adapted and produced on stage and in film in Japan since the Meiji period that spanned the late nineteenth and early twentieth centuries. He has also been appropriated, recycled and commoditised in contemporary popular culture. Even while losing his traditional authority and legitimacy, Shakespeare has managed to survive. The cynical critical discourse fashionable in certain circles does not tell the whole story about the performance of Shakespeare in contemporary Japan. Although limited in number, small theatre companies such as Yamanote Jijosha perform his plays with a strong sense of socio-political criticism and theatrical originality, eschewing the commercial, capitalist spirit that anything goes if the playhouse is full. Instead, these companies present Shakespeare in a manner to which contemporary Japanese audiences can relate, retaining the underground theatrical spirit of resistance against the establishment.

In considering Yamanote Jijosha's *The Tempest*, this chapter has explored the significance of performing Shakespeare in contemporary Japan. Its *The Tempest* reveals to contemporary Japanese audiences the ambiguity of Shakespeare's text by experimenting with the postdramatic and a new acting style. While critically pursuing the meaning and possibility of theatre and performing arts today, this version of *The Tempest* powerfully presents a critical view of the follies of both contemporary Japan and of the world represented in the play.

Although Yasuda refers to Shakespeare's works as classics, we see on stage not an old-fashioned play but a deconstructed, glocalised performance event, revamped for its contemporary local audience. Theatre and performing arts have long been confronting a crisis. They do not generate economic profits and so will neither defeat nor even compete with fields such as information technology and medicine in terms of market economy supremacy. Nevertheless, we need theatre and the performing arts to learn—and to relearn—the value of freedom, criticism and ethics, and we need theatre companies such as Yamanote Jijosha that are filled with a bold spirit of experimentation. We can reconfirm the value of extraordinary imagination on verge of delusion and the creativity of theatre and performing arts thorough the company's inventive performance of Shakespeare's works in Japan and abroad.

Chapter 3

The Last Shakespeare Plays Directed by Yukio Ninagawa: Possessed by the Power of Theatre

In a few years, Yukio Ninagawa, one of the most famous Japanese directors ever, was expected to achieve the great milestone of directing all of Shakespeare's plays in new Japanese translations. Born in 1935, he first directed *Romeo and Juliet* in 1974 and died on 12 May 2016 short of his goal. He would have become the third director to have directed all of Shakespeare's plays in Japanese, following Norio Deguchi (born in 1940, Deguchi directed all 37 plays in just six years, from 1975 to 1981) and Eizo Endo (born in 1950, Endo directed them at Itabashi Theatre Centre from 1980 to 2016). Ninagawa's works have frequently been performed in London and other cities outside Japan, and his productions have received attention from many scholars and reviewers, Japanese and otherwise; while most of them appreciate his spectacular direction filled with bold visual images and original aesthetics, some criticise his interpretations as strange, unusual or bizarre. This chapter reconsiders Ninagawa's directing from both global and local perspectives with a focus on his last three works: 2015's *Richard II*, the legendary *NINAGAWA Macbeth* (or samurai *Macbeth*) and *The Two Gentlemen of Verona*. Although we need more time to evaluate Ninagawa's whole career as an astonishingly dynamic director, we can now discuss his career not as "in progress" but as "closed."

As Alexa Huang rightly puts it in "Boomerang Shakespeare: Foreign Shakespeare in Britain," the Bard "has become a boomerang business in the twenty-first century": indeed he "has been transformed from Britain's export to an import industry" (1094;

see also Hoenselaars, "International Encounters" 1036-38). Among other directors like Robert Lepage (Quebec) and Ong Keng Sen (Singapore), Ninagawa was undoubtedly one of the greatest pioneers and contributors in this thriving boomerang Shakespeare business, though his works have had conflicting receptions.[1] In his obituary of Ninagawa, Michael Billington writes:

> Yukio Ninagawa, who has died aged 80, was a great Japanese theatre director whose work was marked by its astonishing visual bravura and its ability to harmonise eastern and western traditions. His first production to be seen in Britain was a *Macbeth* at the 1985 Edinburgh Festival that left audiences amazed by its dominant image of cascading cherry blossoms.
>
> Later seen at the National Theatre, that *Macbeth* marked the start of a fruitful professional relationship with the producer Thelma Holt, who over the next three decades brought seventeen Ninagawa productions to Britain: not only Shakespeare but work by Euripides, Ibsen and modern Japanese writers such as Kunio Shimizu and Haruki Murakami. The good news, for a generation that missed the famous *Macbeth*, is that Holt is planning to bring it back to the Barbican in London in September 2017.
>
> Holt, Ninagawa's friend and collaborator, said: "He was a great director because he was catholic, all-embracing and open to change and his amazing love of Shakespeare was based on a desire to discover what the author would have wanted." Ninagawa combined, in fact, a profound sense of the past with an experimental flair that created some of the most moving and ineradicable images of modern world theatre.

Ninagawa was indeed global. Despite all the obituaries in Japan (e.g., Tanaka, *Japan Times*) and abroad (e.g., *The Telegraph*) and the great honour the Japanese government bestowed on him, no serious person would claim that Ninagawa's productions of Shakespeare's plays were always great and successful. However, all theatre people must acknowledge his never-ending challenge and passion for directing plays, Shakespearean or otherwise, which lasted until his death. While radically resisting Western intellectual sophistication and elegance in classical realist theatre or avant-garde from an Asian perspective (Ninagawa and Hasebe 240-41, 352), Ninagawa was a director who was intensely possessed by the power of theatre. In *The Power of Theatre* (2013), Ninagawa writes, "A play expresses communication and conflicts among characters. This power of theatre has enabled me, excessively self-conscious and introverted, to manage to survive" (116, my translation). Although his definition of the power of theatre, if true, sounds too plain and simple-minded, that power nevertheless enabled him to direct a large number of plays, Western and Japanese, classic and modern. More importantly, his preoccupation with the power of theatre resulted in a lifelong pursuit of wonder. Ninagawa continued to hope that his spectators would wonder at every element in a performance, theatrical or otherwise. In this connection, it might be useful to recall Stephen Greenblatt's theoretical concept of wonder from *Marvelous Possessions: The Wonder of the New World*. Referring to Descartes's philosophical writing in the introduction to this foundational book, Greenblatt writes that "wonder—thrilling, potentially dangerous, momentarily immobilizing, charged at once with desire, ignorance, and fear—is the quintessential human response to what Descartes calls a 'first encounter'" (20).

In this chapter on Ninagawa, the first encounter between Europeans and non-Europeans is not a topic for discussion. The point is that wonder, then and now, is bound to be the quintessential human response in the form of complex curiosity or affect. It is a strong response; it can thus be an intense, illusionary, inward state. Furthermore, it can indicate a force that the other owns to attract the spectator; it can be an extraordinary force that the other possesses to make the spectator stand still in amazement, confusion or even fear. Ninagawa was strongly influenced by Mikhail Bakhtin's theory of the carnivalesque, which refers to a literary mode that subverts and liberates the assumptions of the dominant style or atmosphere through humour and chaos, and Ninagawa hoped to bring about this kind of complex embrace of wonder— vigorous, surprising, violent or grotesque—to theatre. One of the most vital elements of his preoccupation with the power of theatre lies in the theatrical power of wonder or affect; he was obsessed with making spectators wonder at his work by any means possible, ranging from acting to scenography. In the rest of this chapter, I discuss Ninagawa's last productions within the context of his ideas of the power of theatre and wonder.[2] Although I do not address the question of wonder from the perspective of cognitive science or psychology, the function of wonder or affect is a vital research area in these studies. For cognitive approaches in theatre and performing arts studies from acting through scenography to spectatorship, see Chapters 6 and 7 of this volume.

In an interview with Ninagawa in April 2015, Yuriko Akishima mentions that several British academics and intellectuals have conservative and perennially sceptical attitudes toward foreign Shakespeare productions. Ninagawa replies that he takes their response for granted and that "he directs Shakespeare plays because a Japanese or foreign audience is moved by Shakespeare plays, discovering their selves in his plays" (Akishima 222); in other words, he directs Shakespeare plays so that his contemporary audience can relate in one way or another to the power of theatre or to his theatre of wonder. Ninagawa's achievement lies in the fact that wherever he directed a play, theatres were filled with multigenerational audiences. Furthermore, in a special TV programme after Ninagawa's death, distinguished Japanese director Amon Miyamoto expressed admiration for Ninagawa's "genius of beautifully showing both human ugliness and wonderfulness, or raw chaos" (Ninagawa, "Special Interview"), with great sympathy for the director's professional loneliness and great respect for his lifelong challenge. Ninagawa said that "it is fun for us to encounter in a play the different self that we do not imagine having, and to develop our knowledge of the world" ("Special Interview").

1. *Richard II* with Wheelchairs and the Tango

Ninagawa had two companies of players: the Saitama Next Theatre of young players and the Saitama Gold Theatre of players aged 55 and older. *Richard II* was initially performed mainly by Saitama Next's young players, assisted by several players from Saitama Gold, in a special, empty, small stage inside the Saitama Arts Theatre in April 2015. It was then performed as a full collaboration between the companies in February 2016, who were invited to the International Shakespeare Festival in Craiova, Romania in April 2016, where it achieved great success.

Richard II begins vividly with approximately 30 Saitama Gold players, formally dressed in kimonos and sitting in wheelchairs. An additional 30 younger, tuxedo-clad performers push around their wheelchairs. This unique direction was inspired by the director's seriously ill condition, which forced him to use a wheelchair. Shortly after appearing on stage, all 60 performers suddenly start dancing to seductive tango music (*la cumparsita*) in a simply astonishing scene. The audience sees that the director's obsession with the idea of death as the tango is a kind of dance of death. In a TV documentary, while showing Ninagawa in the wheelchair directing *Richard II*, the narrator tells us that in this work "the director who himself was confronted with death sublimated death" ("Documentary: Yukio Ninagawa's Challenge") to the highest level of an aesthetics of intensity and fantastic beauty, representing the universal history of human death, mortality and a little hope. This shows Ninagawa's theatre of wonder par excellence. As mysteriously as the dance began, it ends, and the wheelchairs and attendants retreat upstage into the dark. A young King Richard appears on an electric wheelchair that symbolises his royal authority. In a later scene, Richard dances the female part of the tango with his cousin, Bolingbroke, possibly indicating that Richard will be assaulted and murdered.

There is no connection—historical, cultural or otherwise—between Shakespeare's play about late medieval English history and the sensuous tango that originated in Africa and allowed immigrants to vent their stress in nineteenth-century Latin America. Ninagawa employed the tango in the opening scene in order to immerse the audience in the world of the play and thus capture their attention in its first three minutes. Spectators are not only amazed by the thrilling scene but also affected by the macabre atmosphere of the extraordinary power of the tango. Ninagawa's concept of players suddenly dancing a tango may have been inspired by his direction of Kunio Shimizu's *Tango at the End of Winter* (1984).[3] More importantly, it should be noted that when he directed Christopher Marlowe's *The Tragedy of Dr Faustus* in Japan in 2010, Ninagawa employed a tango, which is of course not mentioned in the play's original directions; this tango emphasises the "giving and taking of one's life" within the scene; Dr Faustus danced the female part of the tango with Mephistopheles, and this dance represented "death as a climax of desire" (Kawai, "The Significance," 64). *Richard II* is usually interpreted as a thoughtful play in which the man who was dethroned and lost his identity questions the meaning of his being and of human frailty in general. Ninagawa transformed the play into a thoughtful and dynamic play of (homoerotic) desire and death.

In addition to its striking opening scene, Ninagawa's *Richard II* is filled with bold visual effects and scenography. When Richard makes his delayed return from Ireland to England in Act 3, a vast wave sheet covers the stage, and he and the others float and crawl in the waters. The effect is spectacular and shows the fact that no one, king or otherwise, can defeat the overwhelming force of nature. When Richard is forced to give up his crown and sceptre to Bolingbroke at Westminster in the first scene of Act 4, he tosses them away; the crown begins to rise slowly and floats high across the stage until it comes to rest on Bolingbroke, who holds the sceptre. Ninagawa visualises the fact that these symbols of kingship are frail and fleeting. In prison, the self-deposed, solitary Richard meditates on his fortune and on human frailty:

> I wasted time, and now doth Time waste me;
> For now hath Time made me his numb'ring clock.
> My thoughts are minutes, and with sighs they jar
> Their watches on unto mine eyes, the outward watch,
> Whereto my finger, like a dial's point,
> Is pointing still, in cleansing them from tears. (5.5.49-54)

The stage floor is lit here by a large cross. Richard finally strips down to a white loincloth, reminiscent of the Passion of Christ. As Richard often compares his suffering to Christ's suffering, it is no wonder that he lies down at the transverse intersection of the cross with his arms perpendicular to his body within the lit cross. As Barry Gaines rightly points out, many "productions try to find a way to show Richard as a self-proclaimed Christ figure, but few surpass the literal crucifixion of Ninagawa's unkinged Richard." This is indeed an astounding theatrical event.

In the final scene, Bolingbroke appears on Richard's electric wheelchair; however, there is neither real authority nor real glory. Ninagawa brilliantly exposes the vanity and folly of power struggles. Using both older and younger performers in *Richard II*, Ninagawa successfully creates a unique stage of wonder through their chemistry; he modernises Shakespeare's English history play by means of vivid images and speeches that demonstrate that humans, regardless of age, cannot change their desire for power or their fate. The plays ends with another tango between older and younger players, thus reminding the audience of the circular dynamics of history.

2. NINAGAWA (or Samurai) Macbeth: The Legendary Production Revived

NINAGAWA (or *Samurai*) *Macbeth* was originally performed in Japan in 1980 and later at the Edinburgh International Festival in 1985 and the National Theatre in London from 1987 onwards. Seventeen years after its last performance, this legendary work was performed at the Theatre Cocoon, Shibuya, in September 2015, to celebrate Ninagawa's 80th birthday, and it was performed at his memorial event in London in October 2017.

As the production is famous for its huge *Butsudan* (altar) set, we should remember what Ninagawa said about it:

> [The play *Macbeth*] is set within a Buddhist family altar and everything happens within that frame.... The altar is where your ancestors dwell, and the Japanese will talk to their ancestors within this setting quite naturally. It is a link between the living and the world of death. (Quoted in Braunmuller 1606)

Ninagawa shifted the action of Shakespeare's play to a sixteenth-century samurai world in which the lords were warring. Walking through two aisles of the auditorium, two crones go up to the stage and open the enormous altar; in the midst of falling cherry blossom petals, Macbeth (Masachika Ichimura) and Banquo (Satoshi Hashimoto) enter in armour. While this is a dazzlingly beautiful scene, the cherry blossoms in full bloom remind Japanese spectators of both the joy of life and its transience, since life and death are juxtaposed in the altar. The scene represents the Japanese tradition of life and death as continuous, in sharp contrast to Western views of life and death as absolutely separate.

Billington, who admired the production at the Edinburgh International Festival in 1985, writes in Ninagawa's obituary:

> A play that we were used to seeing staged in Stygian gloom suddenly became a thing of wonder and beauty. No attempt was made to downplay the horror of murder: after the killing of Duncan, a dagger stuck to Macbeth's hand as if glued by blood. Even the famous cherry blossoms symbolised passing time and human transience, and the overwhelming sense of melancholy was reinforced by Ninagawa's repeated use of the Fauré *Requiem* and the Samuel Barber *Adagio for Strings*.

Although the main cast changed between the original and later productions, Ninagawa directed the play in 2015 in its original style, as Billington vividly recalls. It is, however, of some interest to know a significant difference between the first international production of *Macbeth* in 1985 and the revived production in 2015. While director Ninagawa, main actor Mikijiro Hira and others were all extremely nervous and stressed about the first production of *Macbeth* abroad in 1985, contemporary Japanese actors can now perform Shakespeare's works at ease both at home and abroad. In the *NINAGAWA Macbeth* programme in 2015, producer Thelma Holt writes:

> Ninagawa is a citizen of the world, like his preferred author. This year we celebrate his 80th birthday and what could be more fitting than a return to Macbeth with Masachika Ichimura in the title role and Yuko Tanaka as Lady Macbeth, both of them already favourites with the London audience.

Tempted by the Witches' equivocal prophesy and Lady Macbeth, Macbeth murders Duncan and usurps the Scottish throne. Fearing that Banquo may have discovered his role in Duncan's murder, Macbeth kills his friend and is later killed by

Macduff, whose wife and children were also murdered. While Hira played Macbeth as a kind of superman in the original production, Ichimura, hovering between life and death, played the role rather realistically, like a contemporary person stricken by self-consciousness. Unlike Komaki Kurihara, who transformed herself into a kind of witch in the original production, Yuko Tanaka calmly plays Lady Macbeth just as she is, which is, in a sense, weirder. Holt writes:

> We are indeed fortunate, for we have broken the barrier of language. We do use subtitles and an English-speaking audience might glance at them occasionally. However, they are merely a guideline, proving that action really does sometimes speak clearly than words. ("Programme of *NINAGAWA Macbeth*")

The original production was characterised by its historical-cultural shift and visualisation so that the local Japanese audience could appreciate Shakespeare's Scottish tragedy, and it worked splendidly for most British and non-English-speaking spectators. The initial shocking impact of Ninagawa's theatre of wonder may have decreased, yet his *Macbeth* remains the quintessence of his theatre of wonder in terms of its theatrical power, its visual beauty and its sheer weirdness (e.g., the huge altar, cherry blossoms, the Witches in Kabuki style and violent fights); there is a kind of dialogue between the living and the dead, or the past and the present, at the altar. Ninagawa's ability to synthesise sound, colour and space remains arresting and fresh, if they are by now a little more familiar. However, we should not focus solely on his spectacular audio-visual effects since he also gave strict directions to the players on how to deliver Shakespeare's speeches, even in the Japanese version. For these reasons, Ninagawa was highly successful in bringing about the power of theatre as communication, particularly in its nonverbal elements.

Chapter 3

3. *The Two Gentlemen of Verona* with an All-Male Cast

Ninagawa started to direct an all-male Shakespeare series in the twenty-first century for two reasons. First, only male players, adults and boys, were available in Shakespeare's age, and second, Ninagawa hoped to produce not only a classic play but also a fresher and more accessible play—or "a new Shakespeare" (Akishima 131)—for Japanese spectators. He directed six plays in his all-male series: *As You Like It* (2004), *The Comedy of Errors* (2006), *Love's Labour's Lost* (2007), *Much Ado About Nothing* (2008), *The Taming of the Shrew* (2010) and *The Merchant of Venice* (2013). As Japanese Kabuki was traditionally an all-male art form, Japanese people are familiar with *onnagata* or *oyama*, male actors who played women's roles in Kabuki theatre. In fact, the highly talented and popular Kabuki actor Kamejiro Ichikawa played Katharina with great skill and a brilliant sense of humour in *The Taming of the Shrew*. However, the all-male series was generally characterised by young players and popular stars in the main roles.

The Two Gentlemen of Verona, the thirty-first in Ninagawa's series of Shakespeare plays and seventh in the all-male series, was performed in October 2015. The main cast included three popular stars: Junpei Mizobata (Julia), Ryosuke Miura (Proteus) and Mitsuomi Takahashi (Valentine). It also included Ninagawa's form of *onnagata*, Yuki Tsukikawa (Silvia). The play is of great interest as one of Shakespeare's early comedies:

> Julia is the first of Shakespeare's heroines in male disguise, a device whose usefulness to boy players Shakespeare would continue to exploit in later plays. Julia's predicament as the servant of the man she loves, employed by him to woo another woman, anticipates that of Viola in *Twelfth Night*, and the name she adopts in disguise, "Sebastian," is that of Viola's twin brother. (*The Two*

Gentlemen of Verona, *The Arden Complete Shakespeare*, 1217)

Employing the device of cross-dressing and disguise, *The Two Gentlemen of Verona* enacts a total confusion of gender (and sexuality) throughout. As its perfunctory ending shows, however, the play is obviously not a masterpiece, and Ninagawa's interpretation remained rather conventional.

In her book on *As You Like It*, Lesley Wade Soule writes that the boy actor who played Rosalind had "charisma," "the uncanny" and "otherness," although we do not yet know much about him, not even his name (112). The boy actor is considered to have had a charm that derived from the tradition of devils and fools in religious rituals, folk or popular festivals and entertainment in the Middle Ages. On the other hand, he probably bore the uncanny characteristic of an adolescent on the threshold between childhood and adulthood. It is improbable to find such radical otherness and epistemological impact as Julia/Sebastian in *The Two Gentlemen of Verona* as directed by Ninagawa. Yet, Julia/Sebastian, along with Sylvia, certainly had a peculiar charm and attraction, so the production was in a sense "a new Shakespeare." Although most of the Japanese spectators were delighted to watch it, I have to admit that it lacked true imagination and insight; it did not fully utilise the all-male cast to shed new light on the cognitive questions and aesthetics of gender, sexuality and homoerotic desire on the contemporary stage.

While Ninagawa's production of *The Two Gentlemen of Verona* was relatively conventional, his effective use of the aisles of the Saitama Arts Theatre is noteworthy. The Saitama Arts Theatre has four specialist halls suitable for staging theatrical art forms, such as plays, dance, music and audio-visual performances. The main proscenium theatre is used to stage plays, musicals, operas, ballets and contemporary dance performances: "The auditorium is the ideal size for conveying the human voice, while the seating layout enables the audience to fully engage in the live experience"

(Saitama homepage). The main theatre also has one of the biggest stages in Japan, as well as the latest in stage machinery, lighting and acoustic technology. The theatre has a total of 776 seats, with 610 seats on the first floor and 166 seats on the second floor.

The structure of this theatre (stage with huge depth and auditorium) is of vital importance for the popularity of Ninagawa's Shakespeare plays. Although he was able to use the large stage provided with the full range of high-tech devices as flexibly as possible, I would like to focus on the four aisles on the first floor. He used the central two aisles as a kind of *hanamichi*, which is an extra stage section used in Kabuki theatre. A proper Kabuki *hanamichi* is a long, raised platform that runs from the back of the theatre, left of centre, through the audience and connects with the main stage. Generally, it is used for characters' entrances and exits, though it can also be used for asides or scenes taking place apart from the main action. In this use, it can be seen as an alley theatre connected to a larger stage. Ninagawa used aisles flexibly and effectively to involve the audience in the play's action. While supporting characters put up props, including a flag of Verona, on the stage, *The Two Gentlemen of Verona* begins with the dramatic entrance of the two protagonists. Valentine, who is leaving for Milan, and Proteus emerge from two doors and exchange dialogue as they walk up the second and the third aisles, thus making the spectators immediately feel part of the play. Many other characters enter and deliver their lines in the aisles as if they were in the streets of Verona or Milan. As he did with other comedies, Ninagawa transformed the whole theatre, both the stage and the auditorium, into a kind of carnival space.

Ninagawa used the whole auditorium (all the four aisles and the spectators in the seats) especially effectively during his productions of Shakespeare's English and Roman history plays, which normally struggle to maintain the interest of the average Japanese spectator. For example, in the famous scene (3.3) of *Julius Caesar*, performed in 2014, Brutus and Antony delivered their speeches to the audience as if it were composed of Roman citizens. For other plays, Ninagawa excelled at casting the audience into the illusory roles of English commoners, involving them in the action of the historical plays as pseudo-witnesses or participants, letting them reflect on the historical similarities and differences between East and West. Ninagawa's use of the Saitama Arts Theatre's structure during the production of *The Two Gentlemen of Verona* was limited; he used it conventionally to invite the spectators to the theatrical space. His use of the theatrical affordance and environment to direct the play and his deliberate method of involving the spectators in the festive space of the play are nevertheless highly effective and entertaining as a kind of immersive theatre.

Although Ninagawa was possessed by the power of theatre even in his seriously ill condition and directed several Shakespeare plays, his last plays were not as brilliant as they might have been, as he was still experimenting with the medium. His concept of the power of theatre as communication seems less innovative in the age of postdramatic, performative and intermedial turns. Regardless of legitimate or questionable critiques of his directing, however, we cannot deny that his bold, imaginative and profoundly visual direction yields fabulous theatrical effects and that his power of theatre immediately and successfully grabs the audience's attention, thus immersing them in the play's world. In sharp contrast to Peter Brook's extreme minimalism, Ninagawa's direction, full of noise and sometimes excessive for ordinary old and young people, emits its magical and subversive power to give the audience vital energy to live in this world of fierce conflicts. While trying to affect spectators' senses along with their minds, he continued to hope to make global and local spectators wonder at the plays he directed.

Chapter 4

Multilingual Performances of Shakespeare Worldwide: Multilingual *King Lear*, Directed by Tadashi Suzuki

Although this book has thus far mainly been concerned with intercultural performances of Shakespeare and global Shakespeare, in this chapter I explore the question of multilingual performance for the sake of the relevance of Shakespeare in the twenty-first century. Multilingualism has been riven by pros and cons in terms of its ideologies and practices in our postcolonial and multicultural age. Considering new multilingual realities, however, the editors of a handbook of multilingualism write:

> Makoni and Pennycook point out the notion of languages as separate, discrete entities, and "countable institutions" (2007, 2) is a social construct. They argue for a critical historical account, which demonstrates that, through the process of classification and naming, languages were "invented" (2007,1). They add that, in direct relation with the invention of languages, "an ideology of languages as separate and enumerable categories was also created" (2007, 2). Makoni and Pennycook point, in particular, to the naming of languages such as "Bengali" and "Assamese" as the construction of "new objects" (2007, 10) and emphasise that languages cannot be viewed as discrete, bounded, impermeable, autonomous systems. Instead, they propose that "local knowledge" is crucial to our understanding of the relationships between what people believe about their language (or other people's languages), the situated forms of talk they deploy and the materials effects—social, economic, environmental—of such views and use.[1]

Researchers working in the field of multiculturalism and related areas have proposed innovations that are guiding linguistic studies towards the translocal or the translingual.[2]

Against the background of this paradigm shift of linguistic studies and its underlying ideologies, the performance of Shakespeare is also confronted with a great challenge. For example, although it was performed as a part of the Theatre Olympics held together with the London Olympic Games in 2012, we watched a fascinating series of multilingual performances in the Globe to Globe 2012: Shakespeare's 37 Plays in 37 Languages at the Shakespeare's Globe in London from April to August.[3] To be plain, it was an international festival project that offered a diversity of performances spoken in a wide range of languages and did not intend to bring any genuine contact or exchange among the languages spoken on each stage; it nevertheless highlighted the multilingual realities of Shakespeare performances worldwide today. Considering the popularity of Shakespeare around the globe, multilingual performances and adaptations like the Bollywood films *Maqbool* and *Omkara* are the norm, not the exception.[4]

Unlike India, Singapore and countries in Africa and elsewhere, where audiences watch Shakespeare's plays performed in a variety of local languages and in English, Japan is hardly a multilingual nation, though we now hear a diversity of languages spoken by international students on university campuses as well as by a rapidly increasing number of foreign tourists. In Japan, the audiences have watched Shakespeare's plays performed in Japanese mainly at commercial theatres or performed in English by British theatre companies or by Japanese students at school. Bearing in mind this basic situation, Tadashi Suzuki (1939–), one of the world's leading theatre directors, is a pioneer of multilingual performance, with his theatre company comprised of members with diverse origins and his collaboration with other international companies or actors in Toga, Toyama, Japan. Suzuki is well known for his system of actor training, the Suzuki method, which combines elements of Noh and Kabuki with Western realism, but it should be recalled that, from the start, he aimed at creating a multilingual theatre that would be able to show the world original performances from Japan. In this chapter, I explore the nature, challenge and possibilities of multilingual performance of Shakespeare's plays by examining one of Suzuki's most acclaimed productions, *King Lear*, performed in four languages: English, German, Japanese and Korean.

1. Tadashi Suzuki and Multilingual Performance

Suzuki founded the Suzuki Company of Toga (SCOT) in Toga Village, located in the mountains of Toyama Prefecture and started Japan's first international theatre festival (Toga Festival) in 1982, which continued until 1999. He also created the Suzuki Method of Actor Training. While the festival was active, many theatre artists from all over the world came together to Toga to practice the Suzuki method and rehearse plays. After retiring from the general artistic directorship of the Shizuoka Performing Arts Centre (SPAC, 1995–2007), Suzuki started a new initiative at the SCOT in 2008, amidst the contemporary dynamics of globalisation and localisation. Its main activities are as follows:

1. To work as an international theatre company, with multinational members, which had never existed in Japan.
2. The company possesses the whole facilities necessary for theatre activities ranging from accommodation and rehearsal rooms to theatres, a fact that is rather exceptional in Japan. Furthermore, it establishes its own rules for operating these facilities that should not disturb the spirit of creative activities and sustains not just a series of international exchanges but an

internationalised community.

3. The company produces not only stage works in Japanese by Japanese actors but also *multilingual* stage works in advance of the future artistic and cultural activities in the international age, thereby stimulating people engaged in these activities around the world and in Japan.[5]

Suzuki founded the Waseda Little Theatre with other young theatre people in Sinjuku, Tokyo, in 1966 and performed ground-breaking plays such as *On the Dramatic Passions* (1969) as a leader of the little theatre movement. He moved the stronghold of his theatre company from Tokyo to Toga in 1976, renaming it the SCOT.

Suzuki's works include *The Trojan Women* (1974), *Dionysus* (1990), *King Lear* (1984), *Cyrano de Bergerac* (1999), *Madame de Sade* (2007) and many others. Since its first overseas production for a 1972 international theatre festival in Paris, his company has performed in "some eighty two cities in thirty one nations" (Suzuki, *Culture is the Body* 142-43). Besides productions with his own company, he has directed several international collaborations, such as *The Tale of Lear*, co-produced and presented by four leading regional theatres in the United States (1988), *King Lear*, presented with the Moscow Art Theatre (2004), *Oedipus Rex*, co-produced by the Cultural Olympiad and Dusseldorf Schauspeil Haus (2002), *Electra*, produced by the Taganka Theatre in Russia (2007) and by the Ansan Arts Centre/Arco Theatre in Korea (2008), *Lear*, produced in collaboration with the Chinese National Central Academy of Drama (2012) and produced for Seoul International Theatre Festival (2012) and *Dionysus*, produced by Chinese players at a local theatre near the Great Wall (2015). Suzuki's activities, both as a theatre director creating multilingual and multicultural productions and as a festival director bringing people from around the world together in the context of shared theatrical endeavour, reflect an aggressive approach to dealing with the fundamental issues of our times.

Suzuki is also a foundational thinker and practitioner whose work has had a powerful influence on theatre people in the world. His primary concerns include the structure or constitution of a theatre group, the creation and use of theatre space and the overcoming of cultural and national barriers in the interest of creating a piece of dramatic work that is truly universal. Amidst the beautiful wilderness of Toga, he has built one of the largest international theatre centres in the world, including six theatres, rehearsal rooms, offices, lodging and restaurants.

The Suzuki Method of Actor Training was created in order to make actors aware of how their physical senses have degenerated in their everyday lives for the sake of their professional acting. It is an original, hybrid training method influenced by Noh, Kabuki, Greek theatre, ballet and other forms. While training the actors' voices and promoting their self-controlling breathing ability, it places special emphasis on the senses of the lower parts of the body and how to move the feet. Suzuki conceived of the method as a basic form of training necessary for every actor in any nation to intensify the degree of concentration and physical and mental energy; in fact, it is taught in theatres and universities worldwide.[6]

2. A Short Performance History of *King Lear* (1984–2006), Directed by Tadashi Suzuki

Suzuki adapted and directed *King Lear* in 1984, based on its Japanese translation by Yūshi Odashima. He wanted to direct the play to show an old man's loneliness and the possible universality of his insanity (Suzuki, *Collected Works of Suzuki's Directed Plays and Scripts I* 6). For this purpose, he boldly deleted or replaced speeches, characters like the Fool and Kent and entire scenes such as the reconciliation between Lear and Cordelia in Act 4.[7] Suzuki put the play in a contemporary framework, making it metatheatrical. The framework is set in a modern-day mental hospital, where a dying old patient is obsessed by an illusion. That illusion is *King Lear* performed as a play-within-a-play. Furthermore, the male nurse attending the patient is reading a book, which might be *King Lear*, throughout the performance. In fact, the play on the stage might be the nurse's illusion.

Since its first production in 1984, Suzuki's *King Lear* has been performed in Japan and abroad with a variety of alternations and experiments. The first production was performed boldly with an all-male cast, but it seems in retrospect to be a rather simple appropriation that was faithful to Shakespeare's play. After its debut, it was changed and performed every year from 1988 to 2006. In this section, based on descriptions by Yasunari Takahashi and Ian Carruthers, I present a short performance history of *King Lear* as directed by Suzuki, with a focus on the productions in the United States in 1988, in the United Kingdom in 1994 and at the Moscow Art Theatre in 2004–2006.[8]

In 1988, *King Lear* was performed by an entirely American cast in English in the United States, by Japanese and American actors in Japanese and English and by Japanese actors solely in Japanese. That year, Suzuki added the nurse as a character throughout the performance as a new framework; the nurse reminded audiences of the Fool from Shakespeare. The American-actor version in English was generally well received. Invited to the Shakespeare Festival in the UK in 1994, Suzuki produced the play with Japanese actors in Japanese, but it was heavily criticised for its speeches and structure. Finally, Takahashi rightly suggests that "Suzuki's power to arouse strong antipathies both abroad and at home derives from his uncompromising questioning of theatrical art" (Takahashi, "Suzuki's Shakespeare (II): *King Lear*," 253).

In 2004, Suzuki directed *King Lear* in Russian for the Moscow Art Theatre, which performed it in Japan in 2004, 2005 and 2006. Suzuki put Edgar in a wheelchair in 1997, and since 2004 the number of wheelchairs has increased. In fact, the wheelchair has become a central image of his production of *King Lear*. It suggests the diametric opposites of both the seat of power (the throne) and the seat of powerlessness.

Furthermore, it reminds the audience of Lear's speech, "I am / Bound upon a wheel of fire" (4.7.46-47). In contrast to the hostile British reaction to Suzuki's *Lear*, it was acclaimed by Russian audiences, which may be connected to a similarity between Russian traditions and Suzuki's approach. Russians continued to translate and perform Shakespeare into their language and employ the Stanislávsky method. Taking artistic risks, both Suzuki and the Moscow Art Theatre continue to undertake artistic experiments.

Describing the performance of Suzuki's *Lear* at the Moscow Art Theatre in detail, Carruthers states that the power of Suzuki's direction is produced by the dynamic physicality of the Russian actors trained by his method and his ability to readapt and activate those actors trained by the Stanislávsky method; the true strength of his adaptation lies in the fact that he managed to combine these two powerful dramatic languages. Carruthers concludes that as it strongly suggests a theatrical reinterpretation of Shakespeare's great work, Suzuki's *Lear* is worth the same level of acclaim as Kurosawa's *The Throne of Blood*, a film adaption that is a globally acknowledged masterpiece of adapting Shakespeare (Curruthers 115). This short performance history of Suzuki's *King Lear* (1984–2006) has shown that he has continued to make bold experiments on various stages, always striving to bring innovation to the theatre arts.

3. The Four-Language Performance of *King Lear* (2009)

Suzuki adapted Shakespeare's *King Lear* to represent a family's collapse and the problem of aging in contemporary society. It has been reformed and modified since 1984 while being performed abroad. In a later (2009) version, Suzuki added female players to the all-male cast. The greatest difference was, however, his use of several languages: German, English, Korean and Japanese.

As noted above, Suzuki often employed multilingual production; he directed bilingual productions in Japanese and English, Japanese and Chinese, Japanese and Korean and Japanese and Russian of plays ranging from *The Bacchae* to *King Lear*. In his 2009 *King Lear*, the number of languages used doubles to four. What is the nature and what are the effects of this linguistic escalation?

Suzuki's experiment in multilingual theatre is closely related to his exploration of the dramatic passions since his early days. In an interview with Satoshi Miyagi, the artistic director of the SPAC, Suzuki stresses the importance of discovering dramatic physicality and makes the significant remark, "if actors properly control their physicality, we are able to watch a play without understanding what they speak. This is a strength of theatre" (Suzuki, *A Director's Work* 76. My translation.) While well aware of real multilingual societies all over the world, Suzuki does not try to represent multilingual social reality on the stage; instead, by putting a variety of languages on the stage, he tries to discover dramatic passions, the relation among body, words and voice, or perhaps the sound, silence and breath that at times can tell us more than words. Concerning the underlying idea of the multilingual performance of *King Lear*, Suzuki says:

> I think in the world from now on it is highly important for us to collaborate on common ground while being aware of our differences. Based on bodies trained by a certain common practice, we should confront one another with our respective different languages....
>
> What matters is whether or not we can trust a person whose energy is burning in his or her body, while watching a person even though we cannot understand his or her language. (Suzuki, *From Toga to the World* 20. My translation.)

Below, I rethink the nature of Suzuki's four-language *King Lear* by examining multilingual theatre experiments in Singapore.

3.1. Multilingual Theatre in Singapore with a Focus on Kuo Pao Kun

Multilingual theatre is flourishing in multi-ethnic and multilingual nations such as India and Singapore; for example, several multilingual drama festivals are held in India. In Japan, the significance of multilingual theatre will gradually be appreciated by teachers and theatre people as part of multicultural education. Having said that, it is hardly popular yet. However, those people born or living in a multilingual society or environment—in a contact zone of different cultures—live their everyday lives surrounded with several different languages. Most might be speakers of a couple of languages but cannot understand all the languages used in their society. They likely understand whatever language is being spoken but not what the speakers in question are talking about. It is easier for people living in a multilingual society to accept the practice of multilingual theatre as a representation of their reality. In Japan, multilingual theatre is expected to have a great impact on those Japanese who take their "monolingual" society for granted by subverting their epistemological framework.

I now briefly examine a case in Singapore to consider the value of multilingual theatre. Kuo Pao Kun (1939–2002), one of the most distinguished playwrights and directors in that island nation, is considered its pioneer. Kun, born in China, moved to Singapore in 1949 and was educated in Mandarin and English. He was also well known for fostering younger theatre people such as Ong Keng Sen, internationally famous for his intercultural direction of *Lear, Desdemona, Search Hamlet* and others.[9] Kun's *Mama Looking for Her Cat* (1988) is considered "the first multilingual play in Singapore."[10] Kun wrote and directed the play, using Singapore's four official languages (English, Mandarin, Malay and Tamil) and three Chinese dialects (Hokkien, Teochew and Cantonese) and a multi-ethnic cast. It is quite common in Singapore for people to mix two or more languages in their daily lives. Regarding theatre, however, people are used to plays in Chinese in Chinese-dominant regions, in Malay in Malay-dominant regions and in Tamil in Tamil-dominant regions. In the past, therefore, people were unable to imagine actors speaking several languages on the dramatic stage.

Mama Looking for Her Cat, performed in seven languages and dialects, posed a number of questions: the gap between old and new generations, the linguistic question of whether or not translation weakens or simplifies the original text, the loss of people's collective memory in the process of socio-economic development. Multilingual theatre is expected to build a new version of pluralism and multiculturalism across linguistic divisions that can be traced to racial and ethnic differences.

What matters is not only how to represent a variety of languages on the same stage but also how audiences divided by language and culture will receive a multilingual play. Singapore became a British colony in 1819, in 1963 it was affiliated with Malaysia and, in 1965, it separated and became an independent country. Ever since, the multi-ethnic and multilingual Singapore has struggled with languages. The Received Pronunciation, which was spoken by educated people in the UK, was the only English permitted on Singapore's stages until the early 1980s; similar strictures were applied to other languages in the city-state. These regulations and conventions have changed in the last few decades, and people have tried to acquire their own national language, a "Singaporean language," the one used in actual daily life. Singaporean theatre people are still striving for this Singaporean language, always experimenting with how best to capture and present it.

The main two questions of representation in multilingualism are how to deal with languages and how to translate them. *Mama Looking for Her Cat* did not expect a monolingual audience. In Singapore, productions that are not concerned much about whether an audience can understand the languages used on the stage are considered successful representations of the country's multilingualism. In fact, nobody understood all the languages used in *Mama Looking for Her Cat*. Pockets of non-communication, pauses or silence are emphasised in this situation. The fact that the audience members could not fully understand the entire dialogue is supposed, paradoxically, to have invited the audience's sympathy.

Singaporean educational institutions employed Mandarin as a formal language and promoted a "Speak Mandarin" campaign, as a result of which Chinese dialects fell out of use in official arenas like television and radio programmes, with Mandarin becoming dominant. As a result, the role of dialects in the vital social exchanges of different ethnic Chinese communities decreased dramatically. The Chinese mother's tragedy in *Mama Looking for Her Cat* is that she is isolated from her Chinese community because she cannot speak Mandarin. Following Kuo Pao Kun, multilingual plays have often been performed, and the next generation of playwrights, such as Ong Keng Sen, have moved radically towards heterolingualism (see Chapter 6).[11]

3.2. The Four-Language Version of *King Lear*: Towards a Horizon of Linguistic Break-Up

I now compare the Singaporean multilingual theatre experiments with the multilingual *King Lear* directed by Suzuki. In the beginning, there appears to be a great difference between the two. The choice of the four languages used in Suzuki's *Lear* bears little relation to historical and geopolitical affairs such as colonialism, diaspora and migration; it was likely contingent on the nationalities and language skills of the SCOT players. In terms of the study of multilingual performance, it is important to examine the interaction, conflict, negotiation and compromise among those multinational and multicultural actors that took place during workshops, rehearsals and performances. In the final performance of Suzuki's *Lear*, however, we found no trace of cultural conflicts. We heard a diversity of languages, but the performance presented us with an artistic unity.

In fact, the audience did not seem to feel uncomfortable with the use of four languages on the stage. This was not only because most of the audience members knew several of the languages but also was due to the effect of the actors' voices under the Suzuki method. In that approach, differences in accent and intonation of the four languages are evened out and "artistically" unified. While the four languages sounded similarly as energetic voices and sounds, which reminded us of *gidayu*, the style of chanting with *shamisen* developed by Takemoto Gidayu (1651–1714) together with the texts of Chikamatsu Monzaemon (1653–1724), the actors spoke their languages as if they were exchanging real dialogue; we could thus assume that the audience therefore did not feel uncomfortable with the unfamiliar multilingual performance. Fundamentally, although four languages are spoken on the stage, the multinational actors perform as if they are not at all aware of the different languages spoken by other characters, and the overall effect was highly dramatic. In the play-within-a play, where the boundary between reality and illusion in the play is unstable, Lear speaks in German, Goneril in English, Regan in Korean and Cordelia in Japanese. In this imaginary royal family, the father and his three daughters speak four different languages. While maintaining artistic unity, this situation of linguistically incomprehensible or impossible diversity develops throughout the performance.

Suzuki's direction is characterised by its independence from dialogues in conventional realistic plays. This production is set in a mental hospital with the old man who plays Lear a patient, and the play of *King Lear* is an illusion or series of illusions that he imagines. The play employs the basic structure of *mugen* Noh in which a protagonist (*shite*) appears in a dream of a supporting character and narrator (*waki*), who is the nurse in *King Lear*, while a narrator relates his memories and dances. In the nurse's dream, the spirits or ghosts of Lear's daughters are supposed to appear and speak "unintelligible words"; in this respect, it is thus dramatically "rational" that they speak "foreign languages." For example, in Act 1 Scene 5, an enraged Lear remembers the humiliation he suffered at Goneril's hands. Goneril (who speaks English) and Albany (who speaks Japanese) appear but never exchange words with Lear. The whole incident takes place in his mind.

Scene 11 of Act 1 is one of the most impressive scenes in Suzuki's *King Lear*. The "Spanish Dance" music from Tchaikovsky's *Swan Lake* reverberates as all the doors on the rear stage open, and six characters (Edgar, Gloucester, Albany, Cornwall, Cordelia and Edmund) appear in the various doorways before shuffling along with the music to the main stage. Goneril enters from stage right, Regan from stage left. They all start to move their hands with elegance but never dance together, which represents their distant relationship. Lear begins to be tormented by his illusion and auditory hallucination. They are produced by his grudge against his family dancing and seemingly happy outside the hospital. When he judges his elder daughters in his illusion, the characters "suddenly bark like dogs" or start to "speak intelligible words." Finally, Lear falls, holding his head painfully. At the end of this scene, with music by the contemporary Slovenian band Laibach's *Krst (Baptism)*, the characters walk away like puppets.

In directing *King Lear* and other plays, Suzuki has explored how actors can present the unconscious that by definition cannot be expressed in words. In any language, the unconscious is expressed only symbolically in fragments: dreams, illusions and linguistic errors. However, that does not mean that it makes little difference if a theatre company trying to represent the unconscious performs in any language it chooses or that it is natural for such a theatre company to use many languages. The point is that the four-language version of *King Lear* is explicitly striving to represent the unconscious hidden in the depth of the psyche that cannot be expressed in words by employing a variety of means, including of course many languages but also silence, pauses, dance, music and lighting.

Suzuki's original and yet universal ideas of theatre arts and his conceptual direction are of vital importance. However, as they have been already discussed in many earlier studies, I focus here on the characteristics and effects of his four-language version of *King Lear*.

In the first place, although I have pointed out above the differences between the Singaporean director and Suzuki, there are in fact some similarities between them. It is a matter of great concern for both to represent the reality of their own society. Unlike Singapore, Japan is not a multilingual nation, but under the impact of globalisation the number of businesspeople, workers, students and overseas tourists visiting Japan is increasing, and Japanese people now have more chances to listen to foreign languages, especially in cities and on university campuses. Suzuki started to stage his works abroad early in his theatrical career and continued to have exchanges with theatre people all over the world, so he is acutely aware of daily multilingual practice in Europe, Asia and elsewhere. He moved to Toga Village in 1976 and started the Toga Festival in 1982; he explicitly intended to make the SCOT "a multilingual theatre company," the first such company in Japan. At the Toga International Festival Summer College held in 1983, actors from all over the world came to learn his method. The SCOT continues to be a multilingual operation, making it quite natural for the company to take on multilingual experiments. As already pointed out, however, compared with multilingual theatre companies in Singapore, the four languages in Suzuki's *King Lear* were likely chosen for artistic and contingent reasons, not to reflect the ethnicities of the audience.

Mama Looking for Her Cat and *King Lear* share another feature; no audience member can reasonably be expected to understand all the languages used on stage. In the four-language version of *King Lear*, the number of people (both actors and audience members) who can understand those four languages is very limited. The average Japanese might understand a few languages, Japanese, English (as the first foreign language) and German or Korean (as the second foreign language). In

Singapore, it was considered realistic in a multilingual play that the audience was unable to understand all the languages spoken on stage. Is this true of *King Lear*? Even though the play does not directly represent problems in a real multilingual society, it can produce a similar situation, as it deals with an old man's insanity, his isolation and his dysfunctional family. It can be peculiarly effective for the audience to watch these threatening realities performed in a variety of languages, including some they cannot understand.

Regarding this second feature, it should be noted that the classic plays of Euripides, Shakespeare and Ibsen that Suzuki directed are (obviously) adapted and presuppose the audience's prior knowledge of the works. In the case of *King Lear*, many speeches and some elements of its subplot are deleted. One short speech is added when the old man speaks to the nurse (2.4);[12] when he becomes aware of the fact that the nurse is reading a book, he decrees that the nurse stop reading it. Fundamentally, however, Suzuki's *Lear* uses the Japanese translation by Odashima, and the audience can well imagine how the play will develop. Even though some characters deliver speeches in a language that many audience members do not understand, they can imagine what is happening on the stage. The play is directed for the audience to appreciate it even though they cannot understand every single word. What matters most is that there are some moments of such dramatic passion in the performance that the audience can "understand" the meaning of a certain speech without subtitles: for example, Lear says in German, "O, let me not be mad, not mad, sweet heaven! / Keep me in temper: I would not be mad!" (1.8).

In the first scene, Lear, Goneril, Regan and Cordelia deliver their speeches in German, English, Korean and Japanese, respectively. Enraged by Cordelia's response, Lear divides his kingdom into two and gives them to his elder daughters, disinheriting Cordelia. The non-Japanese speeches are accompanied by Japanese subtitles. Following this scene, on a music cue, the three daughters stand up at the same time and walk away. With another musical cue, all the doors are slammed shut and all the other characters vanish. As the music fades, Lear is left alone in the closed space. After this scene, Cordelia appears several times with other characters in his illusion, but she does not speak and in the end appears as a corpse. After the first scene, when Lear, Goneril and Regan speak to other characters, the play usually employs several languages: German and Japanese, English and Japanese, English and Korean, Korean and Japanese, and German and Korean.

The exchange between Lear and his daughters performed in four languages appears to succeed on the surface. As Suzuki does not want his audience to watch the entire play with the aid of subtitles, they are kept to a minimum and, at times, they appear later as a deliberate choice; in these cases, the multilingual speeches seem to be successfully exchanged with subtitles as well. In fact, as noted above, the audience does not appear uncomfortable with the fact that four languages are used on the stage. Although the multilingual dialogues seem effective on the surface, they are not successful at a deeper level. Lear can neither perceive the malice behind his two elder daughters' flattery nor understand the true love contained in his youngest daughter's silence. In this scene, their communication fails.

The four-language version of *King Lear* foregrounds the dysfunctional family that cannot understand one another, each member's alterity and heterogeneity more than any of its monolingual (English, Japanese and Russian) versions or bilingual versions (Japanese and English, Japanese and Korean). The four-language version of *King Lear* is a play-within-a-play recomposed as an old man's illusion set in a contemporary mental hospital. In so far as it is a play, interactions between the characters are vital, but their verbal exchanges sound more unfamiliar due to their multilingualism and result in a powerful alienation effect by preventing the audience from feeling empathy with any of the characters.

From the perspective of multilingual theatre, it is important for people with different cultural and linguistic backgrounds to try to understand one another. It can also be equally important to admit that as a hard fact, we may not fully understand other people's ways of thinking and customs; perhaps, even if we manage to understand them, we can never quite accept them. From this outlook, the multilingual *King Lear*, dealing with a collapse of a family that is composed of four strangers speaking different mother tongues, radically represents the incomprehensibility of others and its counterpart in oneself. The incomprehensibility of others and oneself—that is to say, of all humans—is hardly a new idea; it has been tackled in classical Greek tragedy, Shakespeare and Beckett, among others, but it is of vital importance for theatre arts to rediscover it over and over again and continue to explore it.

In order to understand the significance, features and effects of the multilingual *King Lear*, it is worth considering the views of Yoko Tawada, a contemporary writer who lives in Germany, travels all over the world and writes novels and essays in Japanese and German. In a chapter on Marseille in *Exophony: Travels Outside One's Mother Tongue*, she writes:

> I think I have listened to no other language than French for a long time without understanding what it means. Thanks to it, French has come to be ranked "the pure language" in my mind…. When we can communicate with others, we tend to only communicate. It is good by itself, but a language has more wonderful power. In truth, I might happen to seek a language that is liberated from meaning. I went outside my mother tongue and have sought a world where cultures overlap because I might hope to reach the verge of the condition where each language will break up and be liberated from its meanings. (Tawada 139. My general translation.)

Putting herself in locations where cultures and languages overlap, Tawada openly acknowledges the function of language for communication. At the same time, she is aware of its limitation and instead has tried to find new expressions between linguistic meanings and their disappearance (no meanings) and between understanding and incomprehensibility. Both Suzuki and Tawada, who have been active outside Japan, share an idea or vision as expressive artists, beyond differences of professional field, age and gender. Although Tawada presents a distinctive sense of lightness in extremely serious situations in her writing, both artists struggle similarly with languages and cultures and hope to find a horizon of a linguistic break-up. In fact, "the pure language" or "the horizon of the linguistic break-up" must be what all people engaged with multilingual theatre and all people living in multilingual societies dream of. There is only a difference between the way of representing pure language and the way of presenting it; we can appreciate Suzuki's dramatic production of phenomena that Tawada has experienced daily in her travels all over the world.

In the last scene (Act 2 Scene 7), to the echoes of Handel's grave and tragic "Largo," Lear enters holding the dead Cordelia while sitting in a wheelchair pushed by the nurse. All the dead characters stand behind them, on the rear stage. Grieving his dearest daughter's death, Lear himself dies. This is the end of his illusion. Dead Cordelia and Edmund slowly raise their bodies. The characters start to walk away at once, like ghosts. The dead body of old man Lear lies at the corner of the mental hospital like rubbish. As "Largo" reverberates, the roaring laughter of the nurse, who is again reading a book, resounds throughout the theatre. When the music finishes, the stage fades to black.

The old man's family collapse, loneliness and insanity in *King Lear* has a universal, tragic nature. The old man played by a German actor could be a Japanese or any one of us as we grow old. The old man is both the other and ourselves. The "insanity" of our world is also questioned. The audience is suspended, linguistically and psychologically, between understanding and incomprehensibility. The old man, stricken by a grudge, on the borderline of languages, radically represents the karma of human existence moving between reality and illusion, sanity and insanity, self and other, affirmation and negation, and despair and hope.

As a conclusion to this chapter on Suzuki's multilingual *King Lear*, I note the following. In the last scene, pointing at Cordelia's face, the dying Lear speaks bits of words in German, "Do you see this? Look on her, look, her lips, / Look there, look there!" These words seem to pierce our bodies and senses as if they are pieces of a pure language liberated from meaning, even though we know what the words mean. The old man's loneliness and insanity, presented by the actor's well-trained body and voice offering meanings beyond the merely linguistic, overwhelm the audience.

Suzuki is a pioneer of multilingual theatre in Japan. His passion for performing arts has never declined; at over seventy years old, he remains a leader and pioneer. In April 2010 he went to Shanghai to teach his actor training method, and in February 2011 the National Taiwan Theatre performed the musical version of Verdi's *La Dame aux Camellias* under his direction. In October 2012, a bilingual version of *King Lear* in Chinese and Japanese to be staged in Beijing was postponed due to political issues, but it was successfully performed in August 2014 as part of the Theatre Olympics held in Beijing.

In considering the nature, challenge and possibilities of multilingual performance of Shakespeare's plays through examining Suzuki's *King Lear*, this chapter has explored the vital importance of multilingual Shakespeare to his relevance in the twenty-first century. Suzuki hoped to transcend national boundaries with his theatre company in Toga. In his multilingual *King Lear*, he succeeds in creating a great production that does not simply represent a multicultural society but creates an artistic work based on transculturalism and multilingualism and his lifelong pursuit of the dramatic passions. Having said that, the production also presents a limitation, since its multilingual scenes are supposed to be enacted on the inner stage of the insane old man's mind, without any real interaction between the characters.

We therefore might expect a more radically multilingual production towards the horizon of the translingual practice, as is discussed in Part II of this book. The pursuit of translingual performance of Shakespeare worldwide can point to increasing interconnectivities between languages and cultures in this still new century. We need to look closely at the translingual process because that is the area where shared meanings were formed, identities were negotiated, beliefs were expressed, values were reproduced and symbolic representations of reality and order were fashioned.[13]

Reception and transformation specialists in non-English-speaking countries in particular are more acutely concerned with the impact of the multilingual Shakespeare. We try to explore its critical potential to interrogate Shakespeare's relevance in the twenty-first century and accommodate a multiplicity of positions and diversity of voices towards the horizon of translingual Shakespeare performance. Despite all the many difficulties and challenges and anxiety over the excessively global commodification of Shakespeare, we should certainly aim for the goal of translingual Shakespeare performance. Shakespeare is always in process, crossing linguistic and cultural boundaries, moving to other locations, conducting negotiations, changing and transforming both performers and audiences.

Part II

Translingual Performance

Chapter 5

Translingual Performances of Shakespeare Worldwide with a Focus on *Henry V*

An interdisciplinary approach is demanded in contemporary performing arts and theatre studies: cultural anthropology, critical theory, postcolonialism, cultural studies, digital humanities and translation studies are all relevant to today's scholar of the field. We can add linguistic approaches, communication studies, language education and even neuroscience, among others. Part I explored Shakespearean intercultural and multilingual performances; Part II now presents a new approach to translingual practice. Before investigating translingual practice in contemporary Shakespeare performance, it is of great interest to reconsider contact zones in London during the Shakespearean period.

According to Steven G. Kellman, the author of the influential book *The Translingual Imagination* and the editor of *Switching Languages: Writers Reflect on Their Craft*, translingual authors are "those who write in more than one language or in a language other than their primary one"; they are "the prodigies of world literature." Kellman further explains that they "flaunt their freedom from the constraints of the culture into which they happen to be born" by expressing themselves in multiple verbal systems (*Switching Languages* ix). There are a number of such writers around the world from ancient times to the present day: for example, in the English-speaking world, Geoffrey Chaucer, Thomas More, John Milton, Joseph Conrad, Samuel Beckett and Salman Rushdie; Yoko Tawada, again, is worthy of special mention as she has written works in German and Japanese in her significant way of rejecting the idea of fluency (Lennon 21). A very limited number of writers have written works in three languages with equal fluency; most writers had to learn other languages with great effort under special circumstances and have struggled to engage themselves with their creative activities. There are a number of playwrights and novelists with great translingual imaginations, but it is hard to analyse their works in terms of translingual imagination. Since we usually call those who write mainly in languages other than their native languages translingual writers, Shakespeare is not a translingual writer in the strict sense of the term. As discussed below, however, his plays show signs of a remarkable translingual imagination.

When we discuss the subject of a multiplicity of languages or heteroglossia (different tongues), we recall the biblical story of Babel as a source of the original single language shared by all people and the ensuing linguistic confusion caused by God. *Henry V*, discussed in this chapter, is considered "arguably one of the most Babylonian texts in the English language" (Hoenselaars and Buning xiv), with its excessive use of mixed or hybrid languages and dialects. The pros and cons of the multilingual condition have been debated by those who are seriously worried about it as linguistic confusion and those who celebrate it as linguistic diversity. In *Speaking in Tongues: Languages at Play in the Theatre*, Marvin Carlson discusses the macaronic stage presented by Shakespeare and the Elizabethans, who "offer their own often elaborate examples of multilanguage theatre" (36), postcolonial heteroglossia and the contemporary heteroglossia of side texts. Carlson states:

> One of the most important challenges it [the new theatre] faces is the presentation of a newly interdependent world that speaks with many different voices. The heteroglossic stage, for centuries an interesting but marginal part of the dramatic tradition, became in the late twentieth century a truly important international phenomenon. (19)

Chapter 5

This is exactly the subject with which this chapter on translingual performances of Shakespeare worldwide is most concerned.

1. Fundamental Concepts and Facts

1.1. What is Translingual Practice?

In *Translingual Practice: Global Englishes and Cosmopolitan Relations*, Suresh Canagarajah points out that the term "translingual" emphasises two key concepts that have led to a paradigm shift in language education. First, "communication transcends individual languages." Second, "communication transcends words and involves diverse semiotic resources [e.g., symbols, icons and images] and ecological affordances." Semiotic resources are "means to produce meanings" (Canagarajah, *Translingual Practice* 6): e.g., sound, voice, facial expressions, gestures and computer software. Ecological or environmental affordances are possibilities for action that belong in a certain circumstance: for example, it matters whether subtitles or interpreters are available in worldwide Shakespearean performances. Subtitles and interpretation, though linguistic functions, are also treated as an environmental affordance. In fact, in Act 5 Scene 2 of *Henry V*, a French maid called an "interpreter" enters the scene, although she is a comic and unreliable interpreter. In worldwide performances of Shakespeare, non-English translations are often used, and how they are conveyed is as important as what they precisely mean.

Multilingualism tends to emphasise the importance of the coexistence of several languages while slighting the dynamic interaction among them. A study of translingual practice notes the contact of languages and the translingual reality in which we live. It expects not only that translingual performance will represent our translingual reality on stage but also that such a performance will represent, create and evoke a deeper reality than the one of which we are usually aware. This research connects three academic fields that have developed separately. The first is worldwide Shakespeare performance studies, the second is contemporary theatre and performing arts studies, and the third is the study of translingual practice, which has gained importance given the spread of globalisation and multiculturalism in the twenty-first century. This chapter reveals new significance of performing Shakespeare plays and explores theoretical and practical methods for promoting the translingual practice that many people in the world are demanding.

I begin with an example of translingual practice. It is a recorded exchange on the phone between Ahmad, an Egyptian cheese trader, and Hansen, a Danish cheese exporter. Note the word "blowing":

1. Ahmad: We don't want the order after the cheese is uh:h blowing.
2. Hansen: See, yes
3. Ahmad: So I don't know what I can do uh with the order now. (.) What do you think we should do with this is all blowing Mister Hansen (0.7)
4. Hansen: I am not uh (0.7) blowing uh what uh, what is this uh too big or what?
5. Ahmad: No, the cheese is bad, Mister Hansen (0.4), it is like (.) fermenting in the customs cool rooms.
6. Hansen: Ah it's gone off.
7. Ahmad: Yes, it's gone off.

(Canagarajah, *Literacy as Translingual Practice* 71)

Hansen cannot understand what Ahmad means by "blowing." However, it is a serious situation for Hansen, a cheese exporter, since his customer tells him what he can do with his order, and therefore, Hansen asks what Ahmad means by "blowing." Ahmad then tells Hansen that the cheese is not too large, but it likely has been fermenting in the cool rooms at customs. Hansen understands at last that "blowing" is used to mean "gone off." It is remarkable that Hansen and Ahmad try seriously to understand what the other party means. We might recall that there were a number of merchants and traders, English and foreign, in London, represented in Elizabethan plays such as Thomas Dekker's *The Shoemaker's Holiday*.

The main subject of my translingual research is present-day multicultural performances of Shakespeare around the world. I assume that, although translingual practice presents difficulties and challenges, it has a highly significant role on stage and especially in rehearsals, and I also firmly believe that exploring the significance and possibilities of translingual performances of Shakespeare will be of great importance.

Translation studies have recently been flourishing in early modern English literature, and Continental scholars such as Ton Hoenselaars and British and American scholars are actively conducting research. One concept they employ is interlinguicity. Michael Saenger advances "the term 'interlinguicity' to describe a cohabitation of languages that have essentially, never been separate" ("Interlinguicity" 179). He adds in a note that, although he admits the term is similar to Bakhtin's concept of heteroglossia, his "focus is more on the valuation of hybridity in language, a hybridity so pervasive that it renders the ostensible 'unitary language' itself illusory" ("Interliguicity" 196, n.8). As Delabastita and Hoenselaars point out, this notion of interlinguicity "suggests that borderlines between languages are always porous to the point of challenging their autonomy, ultimately also eroding the limits separating literal and metaphorical uses of the translation concept" (13). Although the concept of multilinguality assumes that languages are separate entities, the counterpart of interlinguicity assumes that languages are not separate but intertwined and that European languages are, fundamentally, types of dialects. From this perspective,

Continental and other scholars have shown different insights from those based on the assumption of linguistic autonomy in the analyses of English and other languages in Shakespeare's and his contemporary playwrights' texts, and the development of their studies is profound.

The study of translingual performances of Shakespeare worldwide in this book is a wholly new research field in Shakespeare studies. In analysing Shakespeare's texts, the concept of interlinguicity may well be useful. However, there is a significant difference between Continental and other scholars and the work in this book; while their main concern lies with translation, my main concern is with communication and cultural studies.

1.2. What Are Contact Zones and Contact Languages?

M. L. Pratt, Silver Professor of Spanish and Portuguese Languages and Literatures at New York University and a former president of the MLA, is regarded as the leading advocate of contact zones in the study of modern languages and cultures. She refers to contact zones as "social spaces where cultures meet, clash, and grapple with each other, often in the contexts of highly asymmetrical relations of power, such as colonialism, slavery, or their aftermaths as they are lived out in many parts of the world today" (34). Although her primary concern is cultural contact, it entails the question of linguistic contact and clash.

In *Contact Languages: A Comprehensive Guide* (2013), editors Peter Bakker and Yaron Matras point out that in "some sense, all languages are contact languages: Language is the ultimate, uniquely human tool used to establish and to maintain contact between people"; more specifically, however, contact languages are "languages that have emerged in situations in which the repertoires of languages available to the people in contact did not provide a sufficiently effective tool for communication" (1). There are three types of contact languages: pidgins, creoles and mixed languages.

Although we can add more types of convergent languages in contact zones or language intertwining, the last type (mixed languages) is sufficient for our discussion of *Henry V*, although we must first consider the social and political factors in contact languages.

Contact zones and contact languages must have existed since the ancient period. Medieval London was a multilingual city where people spoke French, Latin, English and other languages, thus forming a dynamic contact zone and producing translingual writing (Hsy 1-26). There were contact zones in London in the Middle Ages and the early modern age, when Shakespeare wrote his plays. Although people used mixed languages in many communities in early modern Europe (Burke 111-40), the metropolises in particular became sites of contact and the clash of multiple languages and dialects.

1.3. A Brief Survey of the History of the English Language

Following the concept of contact zones and contact languages, I review certain fundamental facts in the history of the English language, relying chiefly on Elly van Gelderen's work. Basic modern English words are influenced strongly by French as a result of the Norman Conquest in 1066. After defeating King Harold II in the Battle of Hastings, the Duke of Normandy conquered England and became William I. Consequently, French—strictly speaking, Norman French as opposed to Parisian or Continental French—was spoken by aristocrats and at court, and vast numbers of new words were introduced to the island of Britain. In sharp contrast to the words borrowed from Northern languages (everyday words such as "egg," "odd" and "give"), the French borrowings were of a political and legal (e.g., "state" and "judge") and cultural nature (e.g., "dinner," "beef" and "poet") (Gelderen 9).

In Shakespeare's period—the Renaissance—Greek (e.g., "pharmaceutic") and Latin words (e.g., "emancipate") were much appreciated. England later evolved into the British Empire and colonised regions all over the world. The English language then become influenced by words used in the colonies: e.g., "pajamas" came from an Urdu term for "leg clothing" (Gelderen 9).

What matters in this chapter is that *Henry V* is likely to represent an imaginary condition of contact languages in the late Middle Ages and that the English language used during Shakespeare's period is itself also a contact language. It is not yet wholly a standardised language of a modern nation-state as an imagined community; instead, it reveals linguistic porousness, diversity, fluidity and plurality that verge on confusion (Blank 7-32).

1.4. Worldwide Shakespeare Performances in the Age of Global English

The key points of the English language from the perspective of this chapter are as follows. Although English is spoken today as if it were virtually a common global language, its status is not and never has been secure. In fact, Old English, which came to be spoken in Britain, was a local language derived from a Germanic language spoken by Angles, Saxons and others who came from today's northern Germany. During the Middle Ages, the British were conquered by the Normans, who were not Latinate but a Germanic tribe, and their language was influenced by the French spoken by the ruling class and by the Chancery (a medieval writing office).

The language in Shakespeare's era was a local language in a small island country, and Continental Europeans rarely learned it: "During the seventeenth century English was not much spoken outside Britain, Ireland, and the American colonies, though it had a presence in the Low Countries" (Kerrigan 66). Today, however, it is called global English or world English(es), and it has become a language used by the greatest number of countries and people in the world. We should remember, however, that British English is no longer the norm in contemporary global English; people "tend to consider the original British English as the other language" (Hoenselaars and Buning xvii). Discussing the alteration and creolisation of English in Africa and India in a paper on provincialising English, Simon Gikandi mentions Wole Soyinka's idea of "a strategic linguistic weapon" and adds that "English can be celebrated not as a global drive toward monolingualism but as part of the diversity of and plurality of world languages" (13). He further writes: "Shakespeare's text is defamiliarised and English is creolised" (16).

Without considering the question of global English and globalisation, we cannot consider worldwide Shakespeare performances today. We also cannot forget the great impact of the unprecedented multilingual experiment of the World Shakespeare Festival and Globe to Globe 2012: Shakespeare's 37 Plays in 37 Languages (see Bennett and Carson; Edmondson et al.). Although we can appreciate performances of Shakespeare's works in a wide variety of languages all over the world, it is of great interest to study Shakespeare in a variety of Englishes during the period when his British English is challenged.

1.5. London during Shakespeare's Time

Shakespeare learned Greek and Latin, at least to some extent, at a grammar school in Stratford-upon-Avon. He often listened to foreign languages when he lived in Southwark from around 1599 to 1603 (Nicholl 42); he listened to French, among other languages, while lodging in the house of Christopher Mountjoy's French émigré family on Silver Street around 1603–1605 (Nicoll 17-18). In London during this period, there were a considerable number of immigrants—professionals, craftsmen, tradesmen, servants and others—who came to England for reasons of such as escaping religious persecution, trade and finding work (Luu 121-31; see also Saenger, "Interlinguicity" 176-200). For example, John Florio, son of an Italian exile, became a foreign language teacher at the court of James I. Many foreigners lived on the south bank of the Thames, where the original Globe theatre was built. It has been inferred that foreigners accounted for five to ten percent of the local population in some areas (Luu 91-104), and a variety of languages were spoken, including French, Italian, Spanish, Dutch and Flemish. Since many of these foreigners were unable to speak English fluently, they went to their own churches. London during Shakespeare's era was already a European metropolis and featured contact zones where foreigners and domestic strangers (Scottish, Welsh and Irish) with their own languages, dialects, or accents lived together, likely with ethnic, cultural and linguistic clashes.

1.6. Foreigners and Foreign Languages in Shakespeare's Works

Marianne Montgomery writes that "early modern English 'foreigners' were not people from abroad but migrants to London from the English provinces. People from abroad were 'strangers' or 'aliens'" (6, n. 15). Since the terms foreigners, strangers and aliens were at times interchangeable (*OED*), however, this chapter generally uses the terms "foreigners" and "foreign languages" for the sake of consistency.

Shakespeare's contemporary playwrights wrote a number of macaronic plays, ranging from history plays like Thomas Heywood's *If You Know Not Me You Know Nobody*, Part II (1606) to romantic comedies like John Marston's *Antonio and Mellida* (1599) to citizen comedies like Thomas Dekker's *The Shoemaker's Holiday* (1599) and Ben Jonson's *Bartholomew Fair* (1614). In these plays, English characters disguised as foreigners for their own reasons speak Italian, French, Dutch and other languages or stage foreigners speak in their native languages or (broken) English with the appropriate accents.

Curiously, Shakespeare's canonical plays, with the possible exception of *The Merry Wives of Windsor*, are not set during the England of his day. Some plays are set in ancient Britain (*King Lear* and *Cymbeline*), while the history plays are set in medieval and early Tudor England; even *Henry VIII*, which ends with the birth of the future Queen Elizabeth in 1533, is set before Shakespeare's birth. The majority of his plays are set abroad, in places like Verona, Venice, Sicily, Athens, Vienna, Navarre, Roussillon, Illyria, Bohemia and Denmark. Nicholl rightly says, however, that in another sense, "*all* these plays are set in contemporary England ... Shakespeare's Hamlet is not really Danish and Sir Toby Belch not a jot Illyrian (i.e. Croatian)" (193). Nicholl adds:

> In Shakespeare, and particularly in Shakespearean comedy, real English life as it was experienced by his audience was shown to them through a prism of foreignness, by which process it was subtly distorted and magnified. In this sense the foreign — the "strange" — is an imaginative key for Shakespeare: it opens up fresher and freer ways of seeing the people and things which daily reality dulled with familiarity.... In Shakespeare's mind, one might say, a foreign country was a kind of working synonym for the theatre itself — a place of tonic exaggerations and transformations; a place where you walk in through a door in Southwark and find yourself beached up on the shores of Illyria.
>
> In the great melting-pot of London Shakespeare could hear half the languages of Europe in half an hour's stroll through the dockyards. But to breathe this tonic air of difference, what better ploy than to live in a house full of foreigners? Their voices float up into the thin-walled room, adding a touch of strangeness to the familiar sounds of the street. (193-94)

Shakespeare's plays are thus filled with foreigners and foreign languages (and dialects): for example, broken Russian or nonsense spoken by French characters to deceive Parolles in *All's Well That Ends Well*; Welsh, which Lady Mortimer, Earl of March, is supposed to speak in *Henry IV: Part I*; French by the French Princess and her maid Alice, Fluellen's English with a Welsh accent, Jamie's English with a Scottish accent and McMorris's English with an Irish accent in *Henry V*; Latin spoken by the pedantic teacher Holofenes in *Love's Labour's Lost* and Evans's English with a Welsh accent and Caius's English with a French accent in *The Merry Wives of Windsor*. To give an example of another kind, Dogberry, evidently an Englishman full of malapropisms, enters in *Much Ado about Nothing*, which is set in Messina.

Furthermore, although a famous stranger like the Moor in *Othello* speaks English, his English is stylistically peculiar in terms of his "code-switching; paring an Anglo-Saxon word with a Romance-language import" (Watson 368-73). Shakespeare is supposed to have written several scenes in *Sir Thomas More* as Hand D. It is of great interest that the scene written by Hand D presents the May Day riot in 1517, an attack on strangers by Englishmen. In London, there had long been strife between the English and foreigners, and at last on "2 June 1592 the Privy Council attempted to calm both alien and native sides in the long-standing war over the London marketplace" (Kermode 76). Contemporary English people's attitude toward strangers in London was ambivalent, ranging from hostile to hospitable.

Foreigners and their languages in Shakespeare's plays tend to be targeted as objects of laughter, which most likely reflects the contemporary audience's taste. At the same time, however, Shakespeare was highly sensitive to foreigners and their languages and shows artistic creativity in inventing new words and expressions, making experiments beyond linguistic boundaries.

There are several theories or assumptions about why Shakespeare and his contemporary playwrights used many foreigners and foreign languages on the stage, including Nicholl's idea of the prismatic and lively function of foreignness mentioned earlier. While discussing the phenomenon of multilingualism and linguistic confusion in English Renaissance drama, Ton Hoenselaars writes:

> It is rarely noted that such unfavourable representations of the stage foreigner and his language may well derive their popularity from a hidden frustration among Englishmen regarding the poor status of their own language, and from

the problems this entailed in a metropolis like London that witnessed an unprecedented influx of foreign refugees and merchants during the period…. (33)

The ambivalent status of non-standard English in Renaissance drama. This ambivalence may be captured as follows: why, given the often linguistically xenophobic stance of the dramatists and the dread of a Babylonian confusion, did they import so vast of foreign tongues and dialects into their language constructs? (38)

The Babel myth serves to exorcise the audience's fear of languages and to present that same audience with a feast of languages. Hoenselaars concludes:

The London theatre was not merely a manifestation of the Babel curse, but also a creative language laboratory in which to rehearse and contain the then current obsession with European tongues…. It was equally determined by a still ambivalent stance in England on the merits of foreign language learning. (40)

In a postscript to *Aliens and Englishness in Elizabethan Drama*, which explores moral, historical and comic plays as contributing to Elizabethan debates on Anglo–foreign relations in England, Lloyd Edward Kermode concludes:

Native and foreign language, as used on the stage and in the streets, are themselves equally alienating forces: languages control entry of "foreigners" and determine hierarchies within their native ranks. The plays do the same jobs of national gatekeeping and organization. Could staging the alien really alienate the stage…? For if the stage was already strange and offensively non-English to English reformers and city authorities, did putting the alien on the stage instead *confirm* its status as a very *English* mechanism for displaying the "other" and for discovering and delineating the self? We leap across time to look through these dramatic perspectives, ourselves the alien among aliens. We search for selves that we can comprehend in the early modern and postmodern worlds. (154)

Kermode suggests that Englishness was paradoxically invented and made stable in its constant changeability on the stage by incorporating and even celebrating alien and foreign languages. This self-reflective function of dramatic performance is equally true of our postmodern world.

In *Europe's Languages on England's Stages, 1590-1620*, Montgomery suggests that although foreign language marks distance, "the theatre promises translation by means of gesture, action, and even the English speech of other characters" (6) and that theatre "is interested in the sound of foreign languages, but it stresses not just difference and distance but translate proximity, making foreign languages meaningful and comprehensible" and "plays are interested in comparing English to other languages and investigating the hybridity of English sounds" (14-15). Considering Shakespeare's new words, Robert N. Watson writes: "Clearly Shakespeare's original audience enjoyed his language, not because (as modern readers tend to assume) they knew all those strange locutions, but partly because they didn't yet" (361).

While bearing in mind these theories and assumptions, contradictory or not, the present volume is more concerned with what Shakespeare's plays accomplish by employing foreigners and foreign languages and what effects they achieve in terms of the characters and action on the stage and their relationship with the audience than why they represent foreigners and foreign languages. This chapter aims to find significant moments of translingual practice, a goal for which *Henry V* is well suited.

2. An Analysis of *Henry V*, Act 5, Scene 2

2.1. *Henry V* as the Most Babylonian Text of Shakespeare's Plays

Henry V is supposed to not have been very popular when it was first performed around 1599, but it is now one of the most popular plays in the United Kingdom (or at least in England); it was recently filmed by Kenneth Branagh (1989), and the Globe theatre group performed it in English as the last work of a series in Globe to Globe 2012: Shakespeare's 37 Plays in 37 Languages. That said, since the play appears patriotic or even jingoistic, it has often been criticised. Noticing the disruptive presence of Wales and Welshness in particular, however, Patricia Parker insists that this history play does not celebrate the unity of Britain but reflects the opposite perspective (81-99; see also Burnett and Wray 1-6 and Ivic 75-90). Some feminist critics have questioned the patriarchal assumptions and representations of feminine vulnerability in this play and upheld "Lance Wilcox's view of Henry's wooing as a rape" (Gurr 59). In *Shakespeare, Law, and Marriage*, however, B. L. Sokol and Mary Sokol make the convincing point that the majority of royal and aristocratic marriages were of political convenience in those days and could have been successful (39, 196). Considering Mortimer's Welsh wife in *1 Henry IV* and the French princess Katherine in *Henry V*, Montgomery argues that despite "a triumph of the English language over Welsh and French," their "languages, rather than marginalizing them, make them central to Shakespeare's inquiry into the past" (25). Although Montgomery is positive about Shakespeare's representations of foreign women, Anny Crunell-Vanrigh analyses Katherine's French and critically argues that traces of "insular French in Kate's morphosyntactic idiosyncrasies serve the political agenda of a play chronicling the process that took the French tongue from authority to disempowerment" (60).

Undoubtedly, linguistic choice is political, often reflecting the power distance between speakers: the linguistic is the political. Since *Henry V* is a conquest play, the

English king and the French princess are not given equal status, because of their power and gender distance; furthermore, the French princess is tinged with the contemporary stereotypical representation of stage foreigners. For all this, the play—Act 5 Scene 2 in particular—is remarkable in terms of translingual practice. It employs more foreign languages, especially French, than any other of Shakespeare's plays, presenting the audience with exchanges between languages. This chapter does not aim to offer a new political reading of the play but reconsiders the interaction between languages.

Henry V is considered the most Babylonian text of Shakespeare's plays. The languages used in the play are staggeringly confused or multilingual: English, French, broken English, broken French, Franglais—which is English influenced by French as a result of the Norman Conquest such as "bettre" (better) spoken by Alice in 5.2.262— English with a Welsh accent, English with a Scottish accent and English with an Irish accent.

As for English, there would have been not only a variety of regional and ethnic accents but also a variety of class-based accents in Shakespeare's day. As contemporary performances of Shakespeare's plays show, class accents are now quite dated. It is anachronistic to hear the mistress of a tavern speak in current standard English; however, had she spoken working-class English in the old pronunciation of the sixteenth century, today's audiences, even native speakers, would have great difficulty understanding it. As for French, it is classified into three kinds: French spoken by royals and aristocrats, French spoken in the French community and French spoken by non-aristocrats, the latter ranging from lawyers to Oxbridge students who learned the language from their tutors to soldiers, merchants and sailors. The French textbook that Shakespeare consulted when he wrote his plays is known: John Eliot's *Orthoepia Gallica. Eliot's fruits for the French: enterlaced with a double new invention, which teacheth to speake truly, speedily and volubuly the French-tongue* (1593). It is notable that of "all the French primers, this is probably the most difficult one to use to learn

French, and yet that is exactly what Shakespeare did with it probably because he found the stylistic variety of the text so engaging" (Saenger, *French Borders* 20; see also Kibbee 181-85).

2.2. The Wooing Scene in *Henry V*, Act 5, Scene 2

The wooing scene is set in a room of the French court in Troyes (1420). The French king and Henry, the English king, negotiate a peace treaty. Henry demands the French princess, Katherine, as his primary gain from the treaty. After all the characters except Henry, Katherine and Alice have left the room, he attempts to roughly woo her. In a previous scene (Act 3 Scene 4), Katherine learns English from Alice; it is a typically macaronic and bawdy scene; her command of English is not yet good enough. Using English, French and mixed language, Henry and Katherine therefore exchange speeches that sound serious but are actually hilariously comic. Although the French king and noblemen speak good English, Katherine alone speaks broken English, in all probability for theatrical reasons. Furthermore, although both speakers are royal, the scene is written in prose except the first four lines spoken by Henry, with the prose helping to increase the comic effect. Henry as a male conqueror woos her actively and delivers many speeches. Katherine later accepts his wooing under the condition that her father agrees to it; it is confirmed that Henry will be the successor to the French throne. When the treaty is finalised, Henry announces the birth of the dual kingdom of England and France.

Henry's speeches in this scene are at times domineering, recalling his threatening speeches in other scenes. What he says, however, has enjoyed a somewhat favourable reception. Obviously, Henry is dominant, and his marriage with Katherine is one of convenience; however, he seems to woo her earnestly. As for Katherine, although she continues to resist him, she might begin to be interested in him, even though he is the king of her enemy. Since the wooing scene is written with ingenuity par excellence, the scene presents us with intriguing theatrical sights, cultural and linguistic clashes and, most importantly, translingual practice.

2.3. Allocation of Speeches in *Henry V*, Act 5, Scene 2

A survey of the speeches in the wooing scene reveals that their allocation is peculiar. There are 180 lines (lines 98-277) in total. Although there are three speakers, including Alice as an interpreter, the majority of the lines are spoken by Henry. Furthermore, since Katherine's command of English is very limited, she speaks French, (broken) English and a mixed French-English language (see Table 1).

Table 1: Allocation of speeches in *Henry V*, 5.2

Henry	147 lines		
Katherine	26 lines	Details	
		French speeches	12 lines
		English speeches	7 lines
		Mixed French-English speeches	7 lines
Alice	7 lines		
Total	180 lines		

Strictly speaking, Katherine and Alice speak broken English with a French accent, and Henry speaks broken French with an English accent. This type of scene represents one of the most serious challenges for translators and subtitle writers.

Henry delivers more than four-fifths of the 180 lines. He does not, however, speak one-sidedly; while he speaks long lines, Katherine answers in one line or only a few lines. They exchange speeches, but the number of speeches is very different. Henry speaks six times as many lines as Katherine. Furthermore, Katherine speaks more in French than in broken English.

2.4. Translingual Practice: Example 1

At the beginning of the wooing scene, Henry and Katherine are nervous. When Henry delivers a formal greeting and starts wooing her, Katherine answers in broken English: "Your majesty shall mock at me; I cannot speak your England" (5.2.102-3). Probably, in order to alleviate her anxiety and tension, Henry then starts to call her "Kate" (5.2.107), a term of endearment, and often calls her that afterwards. Furthermore, beginning in line 123, he changes the personal pronoun from the formal "you" to the familiar "thou."

Katherine is particularly careful and deliberate in the beginning, often speaking in French. Considering her anxiety and limited command of English, Henry woos her in a very straightforward and simple manner. She nevertheless does not accept his wooing:

> KING   Fair Katherine, and most fair,
> Will you vouchsafe to teach a soldier terms
> Such as will enter at a lady's ear
> And plead his love-suit to her gentle heart?
> KATHERINE Your majesty shall mock at me. I cannot speak your England.
> KING O fair Katherine, if you will love me soundly with your French heart *I will be glad to hear you confess it brokenly with your English tongue.* Do you like me, Kate? [Italics added]
> KATHERINE *Pardonnez-moi*, I cannot tell vat is "like me."
> KING An angel is like you, Kate, and you are like an angel.

KATHERINE *Que dit-il, que je suis semblable à les anges?*

ALICE *Qui, vraiment, sauf votre grâce, ainsi dit-il.*

KING I said so, dear Katherine, and I must not blush to affirm it.

KATHERINE *O bon Dieu, les langues des hommes sont pleines de tromperies!*

KING What says she, fair one? That the tongues of men are full of deceits?

ALICE *Qui*, dat de tongues of de mans is be full of deceits: dat is de Princess. (5.2.98-121)

Although Henry as a conqueror disturbingly forces Katherine to speak English, two facts are of great note from the perspective of translingual practice. First, both speakers, Katherine with her broken English and French and Henry with English and his limited knowledge of French, *do* try to communicate with each other. They interact, employing not only languages but also semiotic resources (facial expressions, vocal tone and gestures) and environmental affordances such as the interpreter Alice, unreliable as she no doubt is. Second, although subtitles are available for the performance of this scene today, there were no subtitles in the original production; the audience would have been delighted to watch Katherine played by a boy actor and Alice played by a boy player or an adult male player speaking broken English or French with an English accent. It is still uncertain throughout this scene how much English Katherine actually understands, but it is generally assumed that she can understand a little of the language.

2.5. Translingual Practice: Example 2

Henry delivers a long wooing speech, apparently sincere and earnest, if rugged

(5.2.133-68). Pretending to be moved by it, Katherine replies as follows:

> KATHERINE   Is it possible dat I sould love de enemy of France?
> KING   No, it is not possible you should love the enemy of France, Kate: but in loving me you should love the friend of France; for I love France so well that I will not part with a village of it; I will have it all mine: and Kate, when France is mine, and I am yours, then yours is France, and you are mine.
> KATHERINE   I cannot tell vat is dat. (5.2.169-177)

While basing the text of his edition of *Henry V* on the First Folio (1623), T. W. Craik, the editor of the *Arden Shakespeare*, 3rd series, changes Katherine's phrase "de ennemie of Fraunce" in the Folio into "de enemy of France" (5.2.170-71), which is closer to the phrase, "de enemie de *France,*" in the First Quarto (1600), adding a terse note:

> Taylor [Gary Taylor, the editor of *Henry V*, Oxford Shakespeare, Oxford, 1982] discusses whether F's spellings "ennemie" and "Fraunce" indicate that the words are intended as French ones. Since the words are essentially the same in both languages, and since Katherine undoubtedly says everything with a French accent, the question is not one of practical importance. (357)

From my study of translingual practice, it is more interesting for her to use a French word here, although her expression should have been '*l'ennemi de France*' if it were proper French. The point is that the word can be both English and French, exposing linguistic porousness and interweaving. Even if the word was an English word,

Katherine pronounces it with a French accent or happens to speak a French word unawares.

"Is it possible dat I sould love de enemy of France?" Katherine, who is largely reticent throughout the scene, reveals her true mind for the first time here. Christians are taught to love their enemies. Is it, in reality, possible that military friends and enemies who killed each other forgive their atrocities and love each other for the sake of reconciliation and peace? Her speech asks a vital question, while at the same time it shows her incisive objection to, criticism of and resistance against Henry. In a study of translingual practice, it is of great note that the French princess tries hard to communicate her own mind, using a foreign language, forced or not. Her speech is the core of the intercultural conflict in this scene. Although they are kin, they belong to different languages and cultures, and their countries have warred for a long time. Bearing in mind the hatred brought about by wars, how on earth can they reconcile with each other? Katherine's question is fundamental and remains valid today. How can we solve it?

To her good question, Henry answers as quoted above. His English is distinctive. He tries to persuade Katherine in basic words and simple structures. His logic or rhetoric is also idiosyncratic and complacent. He acknowledges honestly that it is impossible that a French princess can love Henry, the king of England who conquered her country. However, he does not apologise to her for his desire to possess France and furthermore insists that he hopes to conquer it because he loves it and hopes to continue to possess it. Furthermore, man and wife are one heart and mind; France is Henry's, but if Henry is Katherine's, after all, France is Katherine's, and Katherine is Henry's. In short, he stresses the mutual benefit of his conquest of France.

Following the lines quoted above, Henry tries to communicate his own thoughts, flexibly using French, if a broken version thereof. This is also a good example of translingual practice. Katherine flatters him, saying that his French, which in fact sounds horrendous, is better than her English. Irrespective of his poor performance in French, she seems to appreciate his trying to speak her native language. Henry continues speaking excitedly, but Katherine does not understand what he says or at least pretends she does not. Irrespective of her blushing or embarrassment, Henry is absorbed by having a baby, while mixing French and English. Katherine then mentions her anxiety that he might deceive her, does not accept his wooing and teases him. At last, Henry's patience reaches its limits. His long speech (5.2.218-43) suggests that, although it is a speech of earnest wooing, his game of wooing is over; since he has wooed her enough, now she should obey him. Their marriage has for all intents and purposes been agreed by Henry and the French king, with Katherine's agreement a mere formality. Thus, Henry demands:

> Put off your maiden blushes. Avouch the thoughts of your heart with the looks of an empress, take me by the hand and say "Harry of England, I am thine"; which word thou shalt no sooner bless mine ear withal but I will tell thee aloud "England is thine, Ireland is thine, France is thine, and Harry Plantagenet is thine," who, though I speak it before his face, if he be not fellow with the best king, thou shalt find the best king of good fellows. Come, your answer in broken music, for thy voice is music, and thy English broken. Therefore, queen of all, Katherine, break thy mind to me in *broken English*. Wilt thou have me? (5.2.232-43, italics mine)

Although his speech apparently stresses mutual benefit and reciprocity, it is actually a threat and he again forces her to speak his language. Katherine becomes obedient at last, telling him that if her father agrees, she will accept his wooing. When he says her father must agree, she makes up her mind and accedes.

2.6. English-French Connection

Many royals and noblemen of England and France during the period of Henry V were related, and French was the dominant language at the English royal court and its legal courts. Bradin Cormack aptly describes the subtle relationship between the two languages in this age: "to be English is at once and with equal force to be and not to be French" (quoted in Crunell-Vanrigh 78). The connection between the two cultures and languages is represented splendidly in Act5 Scene 2.

The historical Henry, who reigned from 1413 to 1422, died young at thirty-five years old. However, in 1417 he decided to use English in his personal correspondence, which is considered to have contributed to legitimising English as the language of governance. Shakespeare's *Henry V* represents the dramatic moment when English becomes the dominant language and England thus becomes an English nation.

However, as the epilogue notes, "This star of England" will die young, and England will be stricken by a long-term civil war (the Wars of the Roses) during the age of Henry VI, born to Henry V and Katherine; ultimately, England will lose its holdings in France. The young widowed Katherine will then marry Owen Tudor, and their grandson will be enthroned as Henry VII, the first member of the Tudor dynasty. Shakespeare wrote plays during the reigns of Elizabeth I and James I. Although in *Henry V*, Jamie, a Scotsman, is an object of laughter, it became difficult to ridicule Scotsmen on the London stage once the Scotsman James was enthroned in 1603; in fact, Ben Jonson and his collaborators John Marston and George Chapman were briefly imprisoned for the controversial views of Scots expressed in *Eastward, Ho!* (1604).

This chapter on the study of translingual practice in worldwide Shakespeare performances has explored two examples with a focus on *Henry V*. As the exchange between Katherine's (and Alice's) broken English and Henry's broken French shows, it ultimately does not matter whether their speeches are grammatically correct. What matters is sufficient competence to interact with people of different linguistic and cultural backgrounds. This kind of translingual competence is required of humankind during any period. More specifically, the two characters' translingual practice in the wooing scene represents linguistic and cultural contact and conflict. Although Henry's discourse is oppressive in this conquest play, the exchange is nevertheless highly significant, first because it provides an interesting example of a word—"enemy" (*ennemi*)—that can be both French and English, and second, because it uses mixed languages as well as semiotic resources and ecological affordances.

The example of "enemy" (*ennemi*) is of special interest since it reveals the instability of differences in languages, cultures and nationalities and their confusion and permeability. It suggests that the boundaries between self and other, languages, cultures and nationalities are not fixed but changeable and that many people live on these changing borders. The example reminds us that today we are expected to live across borders or straddle borders and interact with diverse people while retaining our identities, which themselves are changeable, and esteeming the differences we encounter.

It is as inevitable for people to live on virtually vanishing borders in the twenty-first century as it was in the past. In this regard, Shakespeare's plays, which represent many foreign characters living on geographical or metaphorical borders, are revealing and relevant because we increasingly have to live on borders and be prepared to undertake translingual practice. Shakespeare's plays make us rethink borders and boundaries, without reinforcing or annulling them; we should be prepare ourselves to live on borders as the proper places to live. As for the deeper reality on the stage that translingual performance evokes, the analysis of the wooing scene in *Henry V* not only shows linguistic porousness but also and consequently suggests subjective porousness.

Chapter 6

Lear Dreaming, Directed by Ong Keng Sen

This chapter investigates translingual experiments in *Lear Dreaming* (2012), adapted and directed by Ong Keng Sen, a Singaporean director famous for his intercultural productions. An earlier adaptation of Shakespeare's tragedy called *Lear* (1997) was the outcome of the collaboration between Ong and the avant-garde dramatist Rio Kishida (1946–2003), who was acclaimed for her plays focusing on gender issues in modern Japan. Kishida radically rewrote Shakespeare's play, having Old Daughter—a composite character of Goneril and Regan—not only kill her father but also expel her mother. Although Kishida was interested mainly in the gender struggle and Ong's concern was the play's generational conflict, their productive and extensive collaboration transformed the English version of Kishida's poetic but fragmentary script into a sequence of even more splintered fragments.[1] Ong directed the cross-cultural, multilingual and multinational *Lear*, which premiered in Tokyo, Japan in 1997. This ground-breaking work marked by a diverse mix of Asian performers and languages toured in both Asia and Europe.[2]

In 2012, Ong reshaped and directed *Lear* as *Lear Dreaming*. He reduced the number of players from more than thirty to four, two men and two women, with a team of gamelan musicians. The production was revived in June 2015 in Paris as part of the Singaporean Art Festival. *Lear Dreaming* includes several performative experiments. For example, in several scenes, the daughter is played by a pipa (a Chinese lute) player who expresses her mind through music with English subtitles rather than verbal exchanges with the old man. This approach, characterised by the effective use of music, laser beams and other scenic means, is distinctive and can be called "translingual."

While stressing diverse semiotic resources and ecological environments in *Translingual Practice: Global Englishes and Cosmopolitan Relations*, as discussed in Chapter 5, Canagarajah does not define "ecological affordances" but mentions "a social and physical environment," "the context to produce a text" and "ecological and contextual affordances" (7-10). American psychologist James J. Gibson proposed the concept of affordance at the end of the 1970s as part of the ecological theory of direct perception:

> An important fact about the affordances of the environment is that they are in a sense objective, real, and physical, unlike values and meanings, which are often supposed to be subjective, phenomenal, and mental. But, actually, an affordance is neither an objective property nor a subjective property; or it is both if you like. An affordance cuts across the dichotomy of subjective-objective and helps us to understand its inadequacy. It is equally a fact of the environment and a fact of behaviour. It is both physical and psychical, yet neither. An affordance points both ways, to the environment and to the observer. (Gibson 129)

In "Understanding Affordances: History and Contemporary Development of Gibson's Central Concept," Dobromir Dotov et al. write:

> On the one hand, affordances are very easy to explain; they are the possibilities for action that an environment allows to an animal. On the other hand, the affordance concept can become obscure when one tries to exactly define it along with the notion of direct perception. (29)

Chapter 6

When Canagarajah adopts the concept of ecological affordances from ecological psychology to the field of communication studies, he mainly uses the concept's basic meaning: ecological or environmental affordances are possibilities for action that belong to specific circumstances. Semiotic resources and ecological affordances can, therefore, overlap at times. For example, in theatre studies, a piece of music can both produce a meaning and afford a possibility for action under certain circumstances. The point is that a meaning or action is produced, directly or not, between an object and a perceiver or spectator in a particular environment.

As affordance research is now being challenged by cognitive psychology and neuroscience (Dotov et al. 37), it seems very useful for us to consider cognitive approaches in theatre and performing arts studies, ranging from acting (McConachie and Hart 18-19; Kemp 20, 209) through scenography to spectatorship (McConachie and Hart 18-19). It is highly important to understand scenography, which is defined "as the manipulation and orchestration of the performance environment" pursued typically "through architectonic structures, light, projected images, sound, costume and performance objects or props" (McKinney and Butterworth 4), to appreciate contemporary productions (Collins and Nisbet 139-222; McConachie 50-63; McKinney and Butterworth 1-8) like *Lear Dreaming*. McConachie writes:

> The arrangement of benches, chairs, tables, and so on in the performance area for *Twelfth Night*, for example, "afforded" a variety of possible moves for the actor/characters within the space…. The notion of affordances, in other words, accords with common theatrical practice. Directors consider affordances in furniture and other scenic unit arrangements every time they block a scene. (74)

As discussed in Chapter 5, multilingualism tends to emphasise the importance of the coexistence of several languages while slighting dynamic interaction among them.

A study of translingual practice notes the contact of languages with the translingual reality in which we live. A translingual performance not only represents our translingual reality on stage but also creates and evokes a deeper reality than the one of which we are usually aware. Using cognitive approaches in theatre and performing arts studies, this chapter aims to uncover new significance for performing *King Lear* and to explore theoretical and practical methods for promoting the translingual approach required by many people worldwide.

1. Basic Ideas of *Lear Dreaming*

With *Lear Dreaming*, Ong changed his 1997 *Lear* by focusing on musicians and using a minimal text. Many characters in Shakespeare's *King Lear* and Ong's *Lear* were distilled into one performer and eight musician-performers. Ong's long-term engagement with Noh performance sparked his interest in using Naohiko Umewaka, an expert Noh actor, as the storyteller. Since many members of the group did not speak English, the scripts were written in English, Bahasa Indonesian, Mandarin, Japanese and Korean; the only spoken languages in the piece were Chinese by Wu Man (Zhang Yin in Paris in 2015) and Japanese (in Noh style or chant) by Umewaka. Despite the language barriers, the group collaborated well enough. Ong noted in an interview with Porter:

> With *Lear Dreaming*, the space that we went into, it's like when you're following a singer up to a sublime space or a dancer to a sublime space, and for me, *Lear Dreaming* was very much about that. There are spaces that we still cannot intellectualize. So it's kind of a journey. (87)

While employing the eclectic aesthetics and diverse range of the performers, Ong is acutely aware of the effect of presenting "a sublime space," possibly an ecological affordance, which cannot yet be analysed in adequate critical terms. However, that sublime space reminds us of the "flower" or true novelty (discussed below) to which Noh performers should aspire, according to Zeami. Quoting a favourable review of *Lear Dreaming* in a quality Singaporean newspaper, Porter concludes her essay on *Lear Dreaming* as follows: "Ong's technique of minimalizing the use of words and traditional performance to allow music to do the storytelling had succeeded in unexpected ways as reflected by the audience" (89).

Ong's ideas of direction and adaptation shed new light on *Lear Dreaming*. In his "Director's Notes," he stated:

> I was always aided by an empathy with Noh theatre, an ancient theatre from Japan, which has deliberately kept its cosmos apart from daily life.... For perhaps in the ancient is the contemporary—the purity, the minimal, the rigour. I am searching for this art for life, a new way of living in a media-saturated, technological world that is relentlessly impacted by political manifestos and consumer advertising.

Peterson also interviewed Ong after the work was performed and wrote about it in "Being Affected: An Interview with Ong Keng Sen of TheatreWorks Singapore in Conversation with William Peterson." In the interview, Ong discussed the process of adaptation as it relates to re-imagining Shakespeare in his *Lear* (1997), *Desdemona* (2000), *Search: Hamlet* (2002) and *Lear Dreaming* (2012).[3]

Regarding *Lear*, which was internationally acclaimed but received negative evaluations from some critics due to its uneven hybridity (Alexander Huang, *Chinese Shakespeare* 4-5; Peterson, *Theatre and Culture* 214-18; Yong, "Shakespeare Here and There"), Ong admitted that he was "more interested in this aesthetic expansion coming from juxtaposition and assemblage" and that while trying to hold true to what he perceived as interculturalism, he was involved with the opposite process of complicating and confounding that seamless fluidity (170). Departing radically from Shakespeare's text in his *Lear*, Ong "was concerned primarily with symbols and representations of new Asia with all their ambivalences" (172).

With *Lear Dreaming*, Ong says that he felt called to return to *Lear* in 2012 mainly because he was intrigued by the identity of the protagonist's father figure that he had critiqued, resisted and rebelled against in different works, and he was interested in the father's individual agency and individual representation (171). He was less concerned with the conflation of art forms and culture to represent characters; his interest was "individual agency," manifesting itself in *Lear Dreaming* "through an urgency to represent the dream time of Lear, the individual" (172). Entering into "the sensitivity and vulnerability" of the father figure's dream, he hoped "to tell a different story": "The production was no longer an epic sweep of cultures but the tragedy of a human being" (172). Evidently, there is a significant conceptual and theatrical difference between Ong's two versions of 1997 and 2012.

In the interview with Peterson, Ong refers to Jean-Luc Nancy's idea of *mondialisation*—an authentic world forming—as a resistance to globalisation, which leads to uniformity and injustice (Nancy 33-55). Directed by Ong, the TheatreWorks Company started the Flying Circus Project (FCP), an intercultural arts laboratory in 1996; in 2004, the project expanded its reach to include artists from Europe, North America, Africa and the Arab world, evolving in new directions as the FCP II. In his keynote speech on the FCP II in 2011, Ong explained his reading of Nancy's concept and discussed the FCP "through a close reading of Nancy" (Ong, "Mondialisation or World Forming" 13). Despite its apparent affinity with globalisation, he hoped to argue "that the FCP is a study of world forming, closer to *mondialisation* rather than globalisation" (Ong, "Mondialisation or World Forming" 13).

Regarding the FCP II, Koh writes:

> Through the concept of altering each other (Alter U) and by tapping into diverse, multiple resources, the FCP built communities through communications and interventions. The result: a world of singularities and pluralities, rooted in resistance against the efficacies of globalisation, making intercultural performance a shifting continuum in exploration. (221)

Foundational to the forming of the FCP II, mondialisation has become the leading concept of TheatreWorks:

> Never once resting on its laurels, [TheatreWorks] has constantly evolved in its quest of world-forming (mondialisation) through art which resists globalisation. It attempts to journey beyond identity politics and nationalisation into open spaces of idealism. The art of TheatreWorks continues to prioritise an expanding process of human relationships rather than the unitotality of globalisation. (Koh, cover)

Ong objected to some academics' criticisms of his boldly multicultural, hybrid and deconstructed works (Tan 133-64; Tiatco 532-38) in his interview with Peterson, saying:

> That's been the biggest fallacy from some academics, who think I treat traditional artists as clay to be exploited… the making of transnational theatre or intercultural theatre, or however [sic] we call it, is about decontextualizing and recontextualizing to create a particular world on stage with different individuals. (Peterson, "Being Affected" 173)[4]

In a review, Mahasarinand made negative comments about *Lear Dreaming* due to its uneven fusion. However, Ong does not intend to merge or fuse cultures and traditions by force, artistic or otherwise; rather, he hopes to sustain differences or even discord, just as he says, "I have never tried to smooth out all these rough edges" (175). Ong seems neither to have read Nancy's corpus on Western philosophy, ontology, Christianity, community, politics and aesthetics nor to agree with it in its entirety. Though a deconstructionist like Nancy, Ong cannot take sides with his radical materialism since he commits himself artistically and politically to cultures and traditions in Asia in particular, which are often immaterial and spiritual. Nonetheless, his partial agreement with Nancy's *mondialisation* is extremely important. Furthermore, Ong's principle of sustaining the rough edges effectively produces "real" intercultural theatre since cultures and traditions are constructed by radical differences and by possible commonalities, all while interacting.

Ong has not employed a fixed singular style or method; he thinks that one of the strongest drives of his work is "the question of how to remain affected by people that you work with and also how to affect them" (Peterson, "Being Affected" 177). He goes on to state that this is also how he perceives adaptation, contrary to "[t]he old-fashioned idea of appropriation," which "seems to suggest" that one is "not affected by the original" (177). Ong's strong concern with affect is of great interest in terms of translingual performance, since affect is closely related to ecological affordance, as analysed below.

Ong has indicated his awareness of the renewed academic interest in the notion of affect as elaborated by Deleuze and Guattari in *A Thousand Plateaus: Capitalism and Schizophrenia* (1980): "you are a force that's affected by other forces, and you are also affecting other forces as you're all in this space" (177, 179). However, the concept of affect in the field of performance and contemporary theatre has evolved from affects in the process of artistic creation as outlined by Deleuze and Guattari somewhat further, and the term is now often used as follows: Affect is not an attitude or a codifiable, conscious emotion, but rather between the body and the world that affects it, between the conscious and the unconscious, the visible and the invisible, the manifest and the latent (Pavis 8). This kind of affect is closely related to ecological affordances not only as possibilities for action that belong to a certain circumstance, but also as more complex psychological processes challenged by cognitive approaches.

Finally, Ong is different from Western *auteurs*. In *Lear Dreaming*, he adopts a collective method that allows his performers to influence the creative process. Although it might be at times incoherent and risky, his affective method or style can contribute to collaborative artistic innovation and a fairer world being formed out of diversity.

2. An Analysis of Several Scenes in *Lear Dreaming* from a Translingual Perspective

2.1. Semiotic Resources

Lear Dreaming begins with the highly arresting Scene 1, in which the old man questions his own identity in a Noh chant style in Japanese while he is on the verge of his nightmare, madness or death:

> Who am I?
> I was sleeping the sleep of the dead.
> Sleeping in the terror of a nightmare I cannot recall,
> Now the sound of music echoes in my ears.
> Musicians, cut the roots of nightmare, open my eyes.
> Who was I long ago? (0:05:18-0:06:24)[5]

As the Fool in Shakespeare's play calls the powerless King "Lear's shadow" (1.4.222), the old man's question is one of the most fundamental ones in Ong's version. The daughter answers him by playing the pipa, while lyrics or subtitles are shown on a screen to the spectators:

> Father…You are my father.
> The being who created me.
> Three selves exist within me.
> Obedience.
> Purity.
> Innocence.
> Father I salute you. (0:06:32-0:08:12)

The spectators can appreciate the beautiful but ominously exciting sound of the string instrument and imagine what it tells or is going on in this scene. The explicit and punctuated subtitles multiply the pipa music's effect here, although words are often used to betray the old man. After he believes the daughter's flattery and banishes the silent younger daughter, who is described rather than presented on stage, he leaves to travel to his kingdom with his loyal attendant played by Piterman, a singer specialising in the traditional vocal arts of Indonesia. In this dreamy journey, he meets his mother, who is played by Kang Kwon Soon, a singer specialising in performing Korean traditional court music, and his wife or her ghost, played by Umewaka, who emerges in Scene 4. While the appearance of two female characters who are absent from Shakespeare's play surprises the spectators, both the Korean song and Noh chant of their distress and grief, with subtitles, surely give them a cognitive impact, revealing the old man's hidden truth or mystery in the original text.

Lear Dreaming employs effective graphics, especially Chinese characters, designed by Ho. For example, as the plot develops on stage, "父" (father), "殺" (an invented character that means "patricide"), "眼" (eye), "眠" (sleep), "夢" (dream), "回" (turn), "王" (king), "主" (master), "生" (life) and "死" (death) are displayed in Scene 5. In Scene 9, the daughter issues a command and the loyal attendant is blinded; while the character "目" (eye(s)) is graphically displayed, the attendant suffers in agony. Although those unable to read the characters can only enjoy their dynamic visual impact, Chinese-Singaporean spectators and other East Asian spectators appreciate the visual and emotional impact of language.

The performance employs gamelan and electronic music throughout. Although the unexpected combination of modern and traditional Indonesian music is notable in itself, the gamelan is particularly important; its musical diversity can be simultaneously ancient and modern, sacred and profane. The gamelan musicians are protean performers since they play their instruments, sing songs and dance for a variety of effects ranging from very sad to powerful and healing in most scenes and even comic in Scene 3.

The features on which this analysis focuses (excluding acting, bodily and other nonverbal elements) are the semiotic resources of music, subtitles, graphics and songs and dances played by the Noh master, the Chinese musician, the Korean vocalist, the Indonesian vocalist and dancer and the gamelan musicians. All help recontextualise and re-imagine Shakespeare's play, making it relevant for contemporary audiences, whether a local audience for a specific festive occasion or non-local audiences interested in adaptations of Shakespeare's plays.

2.2. Ecological Affordances

In this section, two related and distinguished examples are discussed: space and laser beams in Scenes 8-9 and 13. The old man wears a mask that restricts his sight and acting. The main action of the play is performed on a very small square stage, similar to the main stage found in Noh theatre. Unlike a large high tech commercial playhouse, this spatial affordance limits the movement of the performers' bodies. However, this constraint also elicits great moments of intensity and depth, differently affecting individual spectators who are encouraged to identify meaning or possibilities by this affordance.

Painfully realising in the climactic Scenes 8 and 9 that he was betrayed by the daughter, the desperate old man goes on a journey, rowing a boat and still wondering who he is. He is showered by green laser beams and accompanied by ominous music. As Porter notes, "scenic designer Justin Hill introduced the idea of using lasers to generate a structural manipulation of the space" (88), and lighting designer Scott Zielinski responded to Hill's idea. Laser beams represent the river, the other world or neuronal circuits. Whatever they might signify, they highlight the old man's absolute loneliness; in Porter's words, "Ong had an interest in the lasers' capacity to interface with the body, and wanted to use this technology to symbolise an extreme distance from flesh, blood, bones, and the organic world" (89). If his idea is correctly grasped, its contradictory content is completely different from the spectator's perception of the two scenes and their affective force.[6] Whatever effect the designers and the director might have intended to produce by manipulating both the lasers and the space, the scenes can symbolise the dynamic interdependence between the inorganic and material sphere of lasers and the organic and immaterial sphere of the performer's mind. Whatever affects, meanings, values or other aspects the spectators might find here, the scenes certainly evoke the experience of a sublime space. Although it is extremely difficult to explore that space, it can be argued that in his dream journey, surrounded by laser beams, the old man looks as if he crossed the boundaries of mind and body, of the material world and technology, leaving this world for another one. The suffering and madness of King Lear in the wilderness and storm is re-imagined and recreated in the experience of the old man. While caught in a luminous and complex net-like space created by lasers, he appears to communicate with them. Laser beams not only articulate the space but are also transformed in their interfacing with the performer. Although the dreaming old man is a deeply vulnerable being, he emits a force or affect so powerful that it cuts through the laser beams.

The term "flower" as used by Zeami (1363–1443), the Japanese author and Noh theorist, can be considered a metaphor for a successful performance in a broad range of circumstances. In his early works, such as *Transmitting the Flower Through Effects and Attitudes* (*Kadensho*), the term tends to refer to concrete visual beauty, but in his later works, such as *A Mirror Held to the Flower (Kakyō)*, it encompasses a broader field of aesthetic achievement. It is no wonder that contemporary thinkers and theorists of performance and theatre worldwide have drawn widely on this elusive concept. As a matter of fact, Patrice Pavis (80) refers to the work of two previous scholars in his outline of the term:

"Under the name of flower, what is sought is the energetic intensification of the theatrical apparatus" (Lyotard 1973, p.98). The actor and representation are then no longer analysed as systems of signs, but as "affects of very high intensity" (99). The flower becomes a convenient metaphor for moments when "theatre magic takes place," for "the rare moment when what the actor is doing and what the audience is doing come to a point where there is a real flow of life—like the act of creation—when out of nothing something is created" (Croyden 33).[7]

At such an unusual moment, the flower can create an ineffable world out of nothing. In fact, in Chapter 14 of *A Mirror Held to the Flower*, Zeami writes that during any pause or interval, "the actor must never abandon his concentration but must keep his consciousness of that inner tension. It is this sense of inner concentration that manifests itself to the audience and make the moment enjoyable" (107).[8] According to Zeami, it is most important that this "particular point represents one of the most secret of all the teachings concerning our art" (107). Ong's empathy with Noh and other Asian traditional performing arts is in all probability related to this kind of intensity or affect and the aesthetics of "flower" in this spatial affordance.

Following a series of tragic incidents from the mother's murder through the episode of the younger daughter's murder to the old man's suicide in Scenes 10-12, *Lear Dreaming* ends with Scene 13, where the daughter appears alone on the royal throne, singing songs and delivering speeches in a darkness that is only interrupted by laser beams. The spectators watch another sublime space. However, there are both similarities and differences between Scenes 8-9 and Scene 13. In the former, the old man goes on a journey, rowing a boat showered by laser beams; in the latter, the daughter compares herself to a boat: "I am a drifting boat of destiny." Whether or not they have royal power and authority, both are equally frail, similar to a boat on the sea, surviving for only a brief span. However, the final scene is significantly different from Scenes 8-9 in that the daughter does not seem to cross and interface with the laser beams, despite her interaction or play with them. She boasts of her power and independence, singing:

> I have no mother, I do not need a father.
> I am a drifting boat of destiny. I am a daughter of the gods,
> You are an old, powerless, ugly scarecrow.
> And I am a powerful puppeteer. Your life is in my hands.
> Die, father.
> Killing you, from the day on I am my own ruler.
> I have no mother, I do not need a father.
> I am a drifting boat of destiny. (1:26:58-1:29:35)

Nonetheless, she is absolutely alone and empty, separated from humanity, materials and nature, with no family, loyal attendant or subjects. The spatial affordance in the final scene emphasises her apocalyptic and cosmic loneliness, thus asking the spectators the ever-unresolved ontological question, "what is a human being?" at the end of the performance.

Lear Dreaming, a cutting-edge and process-oriented performance, is a rare example of a translingual adaptation of Shakespeare's play; it is thought-provoking, innovative and appropriate for a new age. This chapter has focused on nonverbal elements, semiotic resources and ecological affordances rather than solely on verbal aspects, having recourse to a cognitive approach to scenography. The cognitive approach remains incipient, but it is vital for theatre and performing arts studies and for Shakespeare studies as well. Whether theatre companies perform Shakespeare's plays using the original or a translated or adapted text, they may have problems in making them relevant for contemporary audiences. Similarly, scholars cannot sufficiently consider a production of Shakespeare's play if they are concerned primarily with its verbal elements: they have to consider the meaning, value and other aspects of semiotic resources and ecological affordances, including their impact on the spectators. These elements and impact are always changing and can never be fixed. *King Lear* thus continues to offer opportunities to find new meanings, values and possibilities.

Ong's radical adaptation of *King Lear* suggests that when Shakespeare's plays are translated, adapted and performed anywhere in the world or in an international collaboration, the number of languages or words can be reduced and other semiotic resources (e.g., computer graphics) and ecological affordances can be used to affect anyone on stage and in the auditorium. It is noteworthy that *Lear Dreaming* succeeds in presenting several sublime spaces as the deeper reality on stage that translingual performance is expected to evoke, a space that awaits future elucidation.[9]

Chapter 7

Safaring the Night: *A Midsummer Night's Dream* Updated

This chapter discusses *Safaring the Night*, a highly experimental production of Shakespeare's *A Midsummer Night's Dream* performed at a special venue in March 2017: the Sumida Studio Park in Tokyo.[1] It was a site-specific performance, much like Ong Keng Sen's *Search Hamlet*, which was performed at Kronborg Castle, Elsinore, Denmark, in August 2002, and was also a kind of immersive performance, like the dreamthinkspeak theatre company's works or Punchdrunk's *Sleep No More*, performed in London (2003), New York (2011–) and Shanghai (2016–) and directed by Felix Barrett and Maxine Doyle. Yasuro Ito, a promising director and writer, directed *Safaring the Night*. While based on Shakespeare's *A Midsummer Night's Drea*m in terms of plot, characters and motifs, the play, performed by the theatre arts group Underground Airport (UGA), adapted or updated the original for a contemporary, younger audience living in the post-human and post-Internet age. Participants (audience members) were invited to immerse themselves in this high-tech performance and explore its mysterious and weird world (a safari park studio site at night), by employing Safari, a browser developed by Apple Inc., on their smartphones. This chapter investigates *Safaring the Night* mainly in terms of the translingual performance of Shakespeare's plays as a case study, while introducing cognitive approaches to Shakespeare's performances worldwide.

1. Basic Information about *Safaring the Night*

Yasuro Ito is multitalented: he is a director, a stage computer operator, a writer of dramatic scripts and song lyrics, a novelist and a performer. Having his formative experiences in Canada and the United States during his high school years, he co-founded UGA in 1999. The group is characterised by both socio-political concerns and theatrical experiments. Since its first performance in April 2000, UGA has engaged audiences with stage performances, guerrilla plays and fashion shows while creating entertaining works that question modern society. UGA creates socially engaging theatre productions, developing fantasy stories that express their message through performance, the visual arts, music and physicality. Of special mention is UGA's close connection with the National Theatre Wales. In 2014, Ito and two UGA staff members attended Wales Lab, the National Theatre Wales's invitation programme for new-generation Japanese artists. As part of their Wales Lab project, they developed "their production *Red Dragon and Soil Traveller*, reflecting on the Great East Japan Earthquake, the 2011 Fukushima disaster and Wales' relationship to nuclear power" (National Theatre Wales homepage). Ito has been involved in Project Hush 2016/17, which aims to "uncover the hidden secrets of Rhydymyn," a former weapons facility in North Wales, and the consequences of those secrets, including the bombing of Hiroshima in 1945 (Project Hush).

Crossing borders many times for his work, Ito has matured and produced cutting-edge works. In his adaptation of *A Midsummer Night's Dream*, he endorses the idea that the technological singularity—the notion that technological means will surpass human intelligence one day and a new reality will rule, whatever "a new reality" might signify[2]—is near or will eventually arrive, and he asks ethical and socio-political questions about the relationship between artificial intelligence (machines) and (trans) humans.

Chapter 7

In *Safaring the Night*, the near-future world of 2045 is dominated by two giant rival artificial intelligence (AI) enterprises, Oberon and Titania. Oberon has won a war against Titania; the two AI enterprises have finally agreed to the historic integration of their programmes, and a memorial ceremony—a version of the coming marital ceremony between Theseus and Hippolyta in Shakespeare's comedy—is soon to take place. Guest candidates (participatory spectators) in the ceremony are gathered in advance. They enter the special venue either from the Oberon Gate or the Titania Gate, and each of them experiences the play from a different viewpoint. Each group of spectators (12–14 groups, 80–120 members in total) is led by a guide on a visit to this pseudo-virtual reality world of our future. Participants have to complete an assessment test to attend the integration ceremony. They download a special application form beforehand and walk into the pseudo-virtual reality facilities of Oberon and Titania, set up at the Sumida Park Studio on the day. They are expected to enter from their real world of March 2017 into the world or space of pseudo-virtual reality in 2045 by using their imaginations. While reading a QR code with a smartphone and listening to explanations provided by a guide, the participants respond to a series of questions about the play. After the participants watch or attend events, such as a tutorial on World War III, examiners, who are quite friendly, await them and ask generally simple questions or ask them to express their own views. As the audience members complete the examinations, they receive their scores on their smartphones. Although a favourite actor's photo is given to winners as a prize, the point of the assessment is to make the audience members, most of whom are smartphone/digital-game natives, immerse themselves in the performance while also occasionally making them consider the possible results of the coming singularity. They encounter several events along the way. For example, they watch the romantic conflict between two pairs of lovers (i.e., Lysander and Hermia and Demetrius and Helena) inside and outside the venue at night, as if this event is occurring on the borders of reality and unreality (dream or illusion) and of the conscious and the unconscious.

In this play, set in 2045, Oberon, who is supposed to be omnipotent and better than humans, determines marital partnerships. Oberon decides that Hermia should marry Demetrius, and their marriage is agreed to by her father, Egeus. However, Hermia strongly opposes this decision. During the negotiation process for the integration of the two AI enterprises, Hermia had visited the Titania camp, where she met and fell in love with Lysander. In *Safaring the Night*, the romantic conflict between Hermia, whose secret identity is only revealed in the final scene of the play, and Lysander and that between Helena and Demetrius will develop fantastically, as discussed below.

Although the play is based on an early Shakespearean comedy, UGA attempts to engage the audience in a new theatrical experience of a mobile participatory theatre in which spectators immerse themselves in the world of the play and walk around inside the venue. For the idea of a mobile participatory theatre, Ito seems to have been inspired by the National Theatre Wales, which does not have its own playhouse in the UK but tours domestic and foreign sites, including Tokyo, to stage its performances. Basing the play on AI and the evolution of the future at exponential speeds, Ito, the playwright and director, collaborated with Nobumichi Asai (WOW Inc.), a distinguished media artist, employing the most advanced technological scenography and financially supported by the commercial entertainment company Pia Inc.

Safaring the Night was conceived on the horizon of the third boom of AI since the early twenty-first century, with the rapid development of deep learning and the highly controversial issue of the coming singularity. The play's programme provides spectators with a glossary:

> AI: A programme on a computer that is rapidly developing. While imitating human intelligence, it is now acquiring the ability to learn and think and to interact

with itself, and it is predicted that its ability will surpass that of humans.

Oberon: The artificial intelligence created by Theseus, Oberon's full attorney representative, and a super-state governance system. Approximately 90 countries around the world handed over their sovereignty to Oberon.

Titania: The artificial intelligence launched by federations of countries, 80 countries in total, against Oberon. Led by Hippolyta, chairperson of the Federation of Titania. It excels in biosynthesis technology.

Electromagnetic recognition control: While fully grasping the human cranial nerve exchange, it adjusts it by using electromagnetic waves, manipulates memory, and shows illusions.

VR space: Virtual reality space created by electromagnetic recognition control. In 2045, it is used everywhere in society such as in workplaces, schools, public facilities and sightseeing.[3]

Table 2 shows the cast of *Safaring the Night*; although it looks a little confusing, it nevertheless retains the basic features of Shakespeare's *A Midsummer Night's Dream*.

Table 2: Cast of *Safaring the Night*

Character	Block	Rank/Role
Lysander	Titania	A member of the engineering team
Demetrius	Oberon	Special Agent of the Security Department
Hermia	Oberon	Egeus's daughter
Helena	Titania	Secretary to Hippolyta
Bottom	Titania	The chief of the engineering team
Theseus	Oberon	Oberon's full attorney representative
Egeus	Oberon	Deputy Director of the Department of Infrastructure
Hippolyta	Titania	Chairperson of the Federation of Titania

Blossom	Titania	Chief secretary to Hippolyta
Snug	Titania	A member of the engineering team
Philostrate	Oberon	The chief of the engineering team
Oberon group leaders	Oberon	Group leaders
Titania group leaders	Titania	Group leaders
Examiners	Neutral	Examiners

Puck (Robin Goodfellow), a fairy, is not listed as a character, but in fact he is omnipresent as a kind of invisible cyber agent or electron of the Oberon block; as he says in the original play, he can go all round the earth in "forty minutes" (2.1.176); his counterpart in *Safaring the Night* can travel and play at even faster speeds. The main characters and the fairies in the original play are transformed appropriately for this science fiction adaptation. Interestingly and quite understandably, the AI enterprises are equivalents of the fairy world, and electromagnetic recognition control is the equivalent of magic in *A Midsummer Night's Dream*. (We might recall *The Forbidden Planet* (1956), an older science fiction film version of *The Tempest*, featuring Dr Morbius, who is the equivalent of Prospero, the magician.) Oberon, Titania and the fairies, including Puck, are invisible entities or machines in this adaptation, although Puck in particular is always hacking and causing trouble and mischief.[4]

With regard to the fundamental concept of *Safaring the Night*, in an interview and on his blog, Ito expressed his serious sense of crisis concerning the contemporary world ("Interview"). He is aware that there is a great division between those who think AI is a threat to humankind and those who think it is beneficial and should be promoted. Paralleling the magical world of fairies with the dramatically changing world of modern supertechnology and fusing Shakespeare's play and the contemporary world, Ito hopes that the audience will experience both sides of the division between AI advocates and AI opponents. He is worried about the grave divisions among nations and the international community with such as the presidency of Trump and the Brexit phenomenon, and further explains that the keywords of the contemporary world and *Safaring the Night* are "divisions"—cultural, economic and political—and "a possible coming war." In dealing with the subject of AI and directing the play, Ito wonders "if this is the beginning of the night for humankind or if it is the end itself" ("Blog"). Ito tries hard to mirror (or update) the contemporary world in emergent crisis in his play.

In *Safaring the Night*, the audience and indeed the performers can experience the play from different perspectives. The play uses the whole complex: the theatre studio, art gallery, café, warehouse and other facilities of the Sumida Park Studio in order to represent the theatrical space of virtual reality in the play and displays a huge projection mapping on the wall of the rehearsal building. A reporter provides incisive comments regarding the *Safaring the Night* set in virtual reality. The atmosphere creates a decadent future like those in William Gibson's novel *Neuromancer* (1984) and Philip K. Dick's *Do Androids Dream of Electric Sheep?* (1968), which was filmed by Ridley Scott as *Blade Runner* (1982), and we feel it exactly as cyberpunk.[5] Note that the weird dystopian atmosphere of *Safaring the Night* is brought about by its setting in a virtual reality world in 2045, after World War III and on the verge of the singularity.

A Midsummer Night's Dream is "relatively unusual" among Shakespeare's plays in that it does not have an identifiable main source; "rather it assembles heterogeneous materials and links them narratively and thematically."[6] The same is true of *Safaring the Night*, since while adapting *A Midsummer Night's Dream*, it assembles heterogeneous materials like Shakespeare's play, science fiction novels, animations, films (*2001: A Space Odyssey*, *Blade Runner*, *The Ghost in the Shell*, *Matrix*, etc.), video games and Safari applications. In 2000, a British virtual reality version of this play, a collaboration between the Institute for the Exploration of Virtual Realities (i.e.VR, a research group based at the University of Kansas) and Kent Interactive Digital Design Studio

(KIDDS), updated "the fantasy world of the fairy forest" to "a modern fantasy realm of computer games, cyberspace and science fiction" (i.e.VR); however, it remained Shakespearean comedy. *Safaring the Night* appears to be both a little problematic and yet thought-provoking, as we see below. Although it mirrors to some extent the contrast between the fairy world and the human world in Shakespeare's comedy, the opposition between the socialist dictatorial Oberon and the capitalist democratic Titania feels a little dated, like the East-West Cold War model. *Safaring the Night* may seem to betray the audience's expectations of a Shakespearean comedy, but it encourages them to think about their future a little more seriously while enjoying the show.

2. An Analysis of Several Elements of *Safaring the Night* from a Translingual Perspective

2.1. Semiotic Resources

Safaring the Night employs various verbal and nonverbal semiotic resources: words, gestures, images, icons, sound, lighting, costumes, props, analogue and digital media and technology. A mysterious "voice" is heard at times throughout, saying things like "Have you found what we have been looking for?" and "We are looking for the Indian child." The participatory spectators receive a series of mysterious messages on their smartphones as well: "Remember the dream," "Spring up beyond annihilation," and "Wake up." The groups of spectators visit, with their leaders, a world art festival held at a museum, set in a long, wide corridor of a building in the venue, where they watch artistic pieces or installations reflecting the "reality" of the Oberon bloc and the Titania bloc in this pseudo-virtual reality world of our future. For example, a set of male and female nudes with their eyes wholly painted black or mosaic, entitled "Missing Eye," painted by a "lost" artist of the Oberon bloc in 2042, represents information control and a form of marital manipulation referred to as "public mating," which is the mating, as determined by Oberon, of males and females aged 15 and 17 years, respectively. A large sculpture or architectural object, "Wall and Finger," is obviously inspired by Wall, the character who separates Pyramus and Thisbe and through whom the lovers whisper, in the interlude in *A Midsummer Night's Dream* (5.1.126-359) and President Trump's goal of building a wall between the United States and Mexico; this wall, created by a "dead" artist of the Titania bloc in 2042, likely represents perennial romantic obstacles along with the inequality and discrimination in a democratic but problem-stricken world.

In *A Midsummer Night's Dream*, the fairies interfere and make mischief with human characters who have intruded on their territory of the Athenian forest at night. With the one possible exception of the facial projection mapping of Oberon and Titania discussed below, the fairies acting on stage are invisible and inaudible to the human characters, with the comic but uncanny exception of the possibly sexual interaction between Titania, enchanted by Oberon by means of a magical flower, and Bottom, tricked by Puck, with the head of an ass, on the threshold of dream and reality. In Shakespeare's play, fairies are imaginary, mythical and even diabolic entities, and there are basically no exchanges, verbal or nonverbal, between the fairies and human characters. In *Safaring the Night*, Oberon, Titania and most of the other possible AIs or machines are physically or materially invisible and inaudible; in the AI-dominant world, they send their messages by means of electric or neural devices or have pseudo-telepathic communication with humans. Humans can also send their messages to other humans by means of a sort of telepathy. This nonverbal and science fiction-like communication practice is appropriate to this adaptation, and it is also deeply relevant to translingual performance studies.[7]

One of the most astonishing scenic devices employed in *Safaring the Night* is projection mapping. Projection mapping—also known as video mapping and spatial augmented reality—is a projection technology used to turn objects into a display surface for video projection, frequently used in advertising and art, including experimental performing arts and theatre. Asai is an internationally famous creator and designer of projection mapping. One of his representative works is the "Real-Time Face Generator/kagami." The word *kagami* means "mirror" in Japanese, and the work is an installation that features a 3D mirror capable of replicating a person's face in three dimensions. Regarding this work, Asai says:

> Digital fabrication has been predominant around the world as the popularity of 3D printers represents. This work can be included in the trend. The definitions of "thing" and "information" are basically opposite, but they are equivalent in our mind in the age of digital fabrication. In a way, we can say our "existence" is composed of "collection of meaningful information (= code)." In the human body, a spherule called a ribosome reads the sequence of DNA and transfers 20 different amino acids to produce protein. *In the past, we thought that human lives were analogue and organic, which was different from the idea of digital computing. But human lives are supported by the idea of 3D printing in its essence.* Cloning is done by copying DNA. And this idea expands to ethical issues with artificial cloning of organisms, which are still controversial. Experiencing this installation, you may be shocked. You should be one of a kind, but your "existence" is reproduced with this. So, the title "kagami" includes the meaning "you face your 'existence.'" (Asai, my emphasis.)

Applying this idea and media technology, which has been advancing at an exponential speed, to *Safaring the Night*, Asai provides the play with the special projection mapping of two huge faces of Oberon and Titania on the wall of the rehearsal building at night. As the two 3D faces come to be combined and integrated into one, they continue to collide, crash into each other violently and morph into each other; Titania's face in particular seems to suffer painfully in the updating process. This 3D projection of grotesquely morphing and warping faces (or the parts of AI) conveys strong feelings of fear and wonder on part of the spectators. Projection mapping scenes are popular because they evoke the vivacity and motion of nature and other things, and they have also been employed by other theatre companies; we recall the remarkable example of the Royal Shakespeare Company's *The Tempest* (2016–2017), directed by Gregory Doran, which employed digital technology on the magical island for the avatar of Ariel. In *Safaring the Night*, however, the scene is significantly different from others in that it is used not only to produce overwhelming visual effects of vibrant images or to provide viewers with immersive and thrilling experiences, but as an essential part of the action of the play. The animated image depicts the conflict of the play. The victorious Oberon camp and the defeated Titania camp have agreed to their integration, and they have started to integrate and update their programmes. However, the project does not go smoothly because of a series of attacks conducted by unidentified "terrorists," who are in fact anti-AI, human-centred activists, resisting the nightmare or dystopia of AI rule.

2.2. Ecological Affordances

Safaring the Night is a site-specific performance conducted in a mobile participatory theatre, a very unusual environment for both the players and the spectators, which affords possibilities for their (inter)action, captures their attention and heightens their cognition and consciousness. A site-specific performance should ideally be a two-way process: while the work being performed will enhance the site, the site or environment should also contribute to enhancing the work. In fact, on the one hand, the whole venue of the Sumida Park Studio, located in a fairly deserted downtown area, was enhanced and even enlivened by this experimental science fiction-like performance. On the other hand, the whole venue enabled the work to maximise its aesthetic and theatrical purpose and effects. Both performers and spectators walked around and up and down the venue as a whole, moving from a theatre studio through buildings or warehouses by means of stairs or a large elevator that led to an art gallery used for a "tutorial" (lecture) room. Throughout their tour, the participants continued to watch a sequence of mysterious acts and scenes. To our surprise, *Safaring the Night* has several possible endings, as we discuss below. In one version, the ending is performed on the roof of a building at night near the Tokyo Skytree, at 634 metres high the world's tallest freestanding broadcasting tower, thus creating a most appropriate atmosphere for the postmodern and futuristic era of the play. This ecological affordance is vital for Ito to adapt and direct *Safaring the Night*, which is set in the age of the coming singularity. He says, "since it is a mobile participatory performance, I hope the audience will have such an experience that they would not have while sitting in a chair. If artificial intelligence surpasses humans, humans will have a sense of rolling down from the ecological throne" (Ito, "Interview"). In this site-specific performance, the site and work are mutually beneficial, bringing out their synergy.

Virtual realities created by computer technologies are currently displayed on a computer monitor, a projection screen or a virtual reality headset or head-mounted display (HMD). The site-specific performance of *Safaring the Night* enables the participants to experience pseudo- or theatrical virtual reality without a headset, goggles or any other tool and even to move and act in this environment with relative ease. However, as the two AI enterprises experience difficulties with their integration update, the play makes the participants uneasy about virtual reality. The participants are immersed in a frightening atmosphere, at the border between reality and unreality (dream or fantasy), fact (or truth) and fiction and the conscious and the unconscious. Note that there is no difference between fact and fiction in the digital world: there is only digital data. *Safaring the Night*, based on *A Midsummer Night's Dream*, finally comes to question the world of virtual reality and asks the participants to rethink the values of imagination, dream and fantasy.

A Midsummer Night's Dream, like many of Shakespeare's other plays, is open as to the audience's interpretation, as is *Safaring the Night*, a site-specific performance conducted in a mobile participatory theatre. Indeed, the audience members decide its ending by voting, leading to a real-time multi-ending process. They are asked to understand, imagine, think about and judge the play as active participants on the spot to a greater extent than in any other play. The immersive adaptation works to test the participants' cognitive faculty and to activate their imagination.

In *Safaring the Night*, the integration update continues to be unsuccessful. In the final scene, all the players and participants are gathered in the studio space; the players are on stage while the participants are in their seats. The Oberon and Titania camps are still desperately searching for "the child of India." The characters on stage suspect the child might be hidden among the audience. An audience member, whose smartphone display gets disrupted, is suspected, but he denies their suspicions. Eventually, Hermia, who has been near Lysander on stage, stands aside and reveals her identity; she is "the child of India," which turns out to be the name of the code that changes a human being into a superhuman or transhuman. The superhuman is created in Titania's laboratory using its biosynthetic technology. The superhuman is bored with its life enclosed in the laboratory and escapes from Titania to Oberon so that it can live as a human being. Although we do not know exactly when this occurs, the real or original Hermia, who belongs to the Oberon camp and is Egeus's daughter, dies in an accident. Utilising her preserved DNA and overwriting her data (or employing her memory implant), the superhuman becomes the virtual Hermia (a changeling, or rather, a humanoid); nobody, including her father, is aware of this fact. When the virtual Hermia visits the Titania camp to join a negotiation for the two camps' integration, she meets Lysander; the two youngsters fall in love, just like Romeo and Juliet. In the Oberon camp, the virtual Hermia must obey Oberon's decision and marry Demetrius; Hermia and Lysander therefore elope.

Although *Safaring the Night* departs from *A Midsummer Night's Dream* here, the superhuman (humanoid) Hermia experiences unique distress. She wonders if had she been given an intelligence superior to humans, it would have been meaningless for her to live unless life was accompanied with "meaning." In other words, she asks an ontological-scientific question, the "so-called 'hard problem' of consciousness" (Cefalu 2): can a humanoid have a mind? The distinction between human beings and AI at present lies in the fact that AI has no mind like human beings do, although it is difficult to define exactly what the mind, being immaterial and invisible, is, or what the meaning of life is.[8] Eventually, the superhuman Hermia asks the spectators to choose a future: is it better to live as a humanoid in the AI-dominated world than as a normal human in a human-centred world? The audience must select a Yes or No response in the application.

The ending of *Safaring the Night* varies according to the result of the audience's vote; the play adopts a real-time multi-ending approach. In theory, the votes can yield three results: Yes, No, or a Draw. I saw the play three times and the results were as follows: 49% Yes vs. 51% No on 1 March 2017; 50% vs. 50% on 3 March; 37% Yes vs. 63% No on 6 March. When the majority chooses No, Hermia dies, like a clone or replicant in *Blade Runner*, in Lysander's arms. When the result is a draw, Hermia survives, but we do not know what will happen to her and Lysander. Although I did not see it, when AI rule is chosen humans will have to disappear or be transformed into humanoids. It is cheerfully relevant to find out towards the end of the play that the anti-AI terrorists are actually engineers named such as Bottom and Snug—the artisans from Shakespeare's play—from the Oberon and Titania camps.

In the penultimate moment, however, just as the young lovers (except

Demetrius), Bottom and the fairy queen are released from magic in the original play, the electromagnetic recognition control that had been placed on the characters of both camps in the science fiction adaptation is suddenly cancelled, and they wake up from a dream, good or bad. They return from virtual reality in 2045 to their real world in 2017. All the characters and the audience wake up and are confused, just like their counterparts in Shakespeare's play:

> HERMIA Methinks I see these things with parted eye,
> When everything seems double.
> HELENA   So methinks;
> And I have found Demetrius, like a jewel
> Mine own, and not mine own.
> DEMETRIUS   Are you sure
> That we are awake? It seems to me
> That yet we sleep, we dream. (4.1.188-193)

In *Safaring the Night*, however, remembering a sequence of fearful incidents and wondering whether or not they really happened, Theseus and Hippolyta change their minds; they stop the integration of Oberon and Titania and decide to reconsider their future. Although the marriage between the virtual Hermia and Lysander is not likely to occur, Helena and Demetrius will get married; in *A Midsummer Night's Dream*, Demetrius remains enchanted by magic and marries Helena, whereas in *Safaring the Night*, he is liberated from the electromagnetic recognition control, seems to remember his love for Helena and will marry her. *Safaring the Night* ends with the whole cast of characters dancing and singing. It is not a hilarious comedy but a good play, speculative and thought-provoking.

Safaring the Night reaffirms the importance of imagination. Should the singularity be realised in the future and even if AI has a mind, consciousness and sensibility, it would be extremely hard for AI to have human imagination, since each human imagination is profoundly different, personal: in a word, unique. Human imagination is hard for machines to duplicate. In the original play, Theseus derides the faculty of imagination and dream:

> The lunatic, the lover, and the poet
> Are of imagination all compact.
> One sees more devils than vast hell can hold:
> That is the madman. The lover, all as frantic,
> Sees Helen's beauty in a brow of Egypt.
> The poet's eye, in a fine frenzy rolling,
> Doth glance from heaven to earth, from earth to heaven;
> And as imagination bodies forth
> The forms of things unknown, the poet's pen
> Turns them to shapes, and gives to airy nothing
> A local habitation and a name. (5.1.7-17)

In his introduction to the *Arden* text, while offering a note on the word "imagination" as "in the old sense: the faculty of recalling and reordering visual impressions or images planted in the mind, perhaps to create unreal creatures and objects," Chaudhuri writes:

> A dream is illusory and ephemeral. Yet it engages deeply with reality, in forms that seem alien and unreal because they stem from the hidden reaches of the mind.... In Shakespeare's age no less than our own, a dream could be viewed as a sign, the surrogate for a reality outside itself, a hidden unconscious world briefly brought to surface.... Theseus recognizes this but misses the point in his

celebrated speech on the lunatic, the lover and the poet. In truth, the heightened representation of reality can only be ephemeral, attained in spells, thus apparently *lacking* in sustained reality. (77)

Raphael Lynne also points out Theseus's mental resistance: "Theseus resists the poetics of mind. He does not want to admit a metaphorical tendency in the apprehension of reality, or an exploratory, cognitive quality to the language out of which his world, and the play, are constructed" (105). As both Chaudhuri and Lynne argue, Theseus's famous speech in the original play betrays his cognitive limitations; we can know reality only through strange or unreal forms, such as a dream, stemming from the hidden depths of the mind. What matters most in the original play is precisely that it shows the audience an ephemeral reality through the theatrical and imaginary representations of a dream of love, hate and desire.

With regard to reaffirming the importance of imagination and dream, *Safaring the Night* is faithful to the spirit of the original play. Furthermore, the special urban environment of this site-specific performance of the virtual reality version of the original play increases the audience's deeper engagement with the performance while evoking that ephemeral reality, hidden in the mind, and inviting or stimulating cognitive reflections among both the audience and the performers.

Safaring the Night, a science fiction adaptation of *A Midsummer Night's Dream*, is a cutting-edge and process-oriented performance. It is speculative, thought-provoking, innovative and entertaining yet also seriously critical and appropriate to the digital age. This chapter has considered the factors of semiotic resources and ecological affordances in the play as a translingual performance, with a focus on the breath-taking projection mapping and a site-specific or site-responsive performance conducted in a mobile, participatory, immersive theatre. This performance is realised by means of innovative digital technologies and ideas. While reflecting many elements of science fiction films like *The Matrix* trilogy (2000–2003), *Safaring the Night* (2017) utilises the latest social network systems and allows close interaction between the performers and spectators (or participants). *Safaring the Night* is critically conscious of the issue of the possible outcome of the singularity in the predicted near future. While the spectators enjoy the "in-movie experience" of watching the special features of *Matrix Reloaded* (2003), *Matrix Revolutions* (2003), *Blade Runner 2049* (2017) and *Ready Player One* (2018), they only enjoy those films as passive spectators.[9] In *Safaring the Night*, the audience members are asked to take part in an assessment test as members of a group, and they must follow their leader and assess part of or the entire performance. Their responses are collected and examined by the theatre group. Although we must consider the terror of the invisible surveillance society in which we live, the audience members are expected to be highly active, ethical and thoughtful agents in this performance.

A good adaptation expands the potential of the original. *Safaring the Night* might seem slightly questionable, particularly in terms of changing Hermia to a humanoid in virtual reality; we really do not know what will happen to Hermia (a humanoid character) and Lysander (a human character) on their return to the "real" world of 2017. Their fate is puzzlingly open-ended. While some might think this transformation is far-fetched, it is nevertheless fantastic and relevant, especially for a contemporary younger digital/smartphone native audience. Overall, the play is a fascinating updated version of *A Midsummer Night's Dream*.

Conclusion

This book has investigated a selection of multilingual, intercultural and translingual performances of Shakespeare found mostly in Japan. The first three chapters broadly discussed intercultural performances of Shakespeare: a Japanese-Korean international collaboration on *Othello*, Yamanote Jijosha's deconstructed and glocalised performance of *The Tempest* and the last Shakespeare plays directed by Yukio Ninagawa, which were characterised by magical and subversive power.

Since it is becoming increasingly urgent to develop and enhance intercultural competence and sensitivity in this age of political chaos and crisis, it is necessary to reconsider the intercultural performances of Shakespeare's plays in many parts of the world and enable the performance of Shakespeare's plays with a focus on developing cultural understanding. It is also important to promote cultural exchange through the intercultural performances of Shakespeare's plays.

The fourth chapter investigated the nature, challenges and possibilities of the multilingual performance of Shakespeare's plays through an examination of Suzuki's *King Lear*. It explored the vital impact of multilingual Shakespeare on the relevance of Shakespeare in the twenty-first century. Suzuki hoped to transcend national boundaries with his theatre company in Toga. In his multilingual *King Lear*, he succeeds in creating an incredible production that not only reflects a multicultural society but also represents an artistic work, based on his own transculturalism and multilingualism, in pursuit of his lifelong dramatic passions. Therefore, we should expect more radically multilingual productions. Reception and transformation specialists in non-English-speaking countries in particular are becoming more acutely aware of the impact of multilingual Shakespeare.

The fifth chapter discussed translingual practice with a focus on Shakespeare's *Henry V*. The pursuit of translingual performance of Shakespeare worldwide points to increasing interconnectivities between languages and cultures in this century. The sixth chapter dealt with Ong's radical adaptation of *King Lear*, a rare example of a translingual performance of Shakespeare's play. It suggested that when we translate, adapt and perform Shakespeare's plays around the globe or through international collaboration, we can reduce the number of languages or words used and can instead employ other semiotic resources (e.g., computer graphics) and ecological affordances to affect both stage players and audience members.

The seventh chapter discussed *Safaring the Night*, directed by Ito. This chapter considered several factors related to semiotic resources and ecological affordance in the play as a translingual performance. It also paid particular attention to the play's astonishing projection mapping and site-specific performance conducted in a mobile, interactive theatre. While some might find this transformation extreme and far-fetched, it was nevertheless fantastic and especially relevant to a contemporary younger audience of digital natives; it represents a fascinating updated version of *A Midsummer Night's Dream*.

Shakespeare's works will continue to be adapted, recycled and updated for a variety of audiences worldwide, thus giving life to new performative forms and meanings—whether intercultural, multilingual or translingual. It is inevitable that people will continue to live on the edges of virtually vanishing borders in the twenty-first century, just as they have in the past. In this regard, those of Shakespeare's plays that represent foreign characters living on borders—both geographical and metaphorical—are relevant and suggestive for us, Japanese or not, because we will have to live more on and across borders and be prepared to engage in translingual practice. Shakespeare's plays make us rethink borders and boundaries without either reinforcing or removing them; in all probability, we should be prepared to live and negotiate on borders or in virtually borderless places. We should avoid seeking out easy answers and instead explore a real solution in the midst of our connectivity and contradictions at the risk of encountering the Babylonian linguistic confusion of our digital age. Shakespeare's works are always in process, crossing linguistic and cultural boundaries, moving to other locations and negotiating, changing and transforming performers and audiences.

We try to explore Shakespeare's critical potential to interrogate his works' relevance in the twenty-first century and to accommodate a multiplicity of positions and diversity of voices regarding the concept of a translingual Shakespeare performance in Japan and beyond. Despite encountering the many difficulties, challenges and anxieties related to the excessively global commodification of Shakespeare, we should aim for the goal of achieving a translingual Shakespeare performance through engaging with a variety of new approaches and technologies, such as cognitive approaches, neuroscience and digital technology.

Appendix:
Performance Review: *Sandaime Richard*, written by Hideki Noda and directed by Ong Keng Sen. Performed in Japanese, English and Indonesian, with Japanese and English Subtitles.

Produced by Shizuoka Performing Arts Center (SPAC),
2016 International Festival, Shizuoka, Japan.
Co-produced by Tokyo Metropolitan Theatre and Singapore International
Festival of Arts (SIFA), 1 May 2016.

Wondering why Shakespeare portrayed Richard III and Shylock as such damnable villains, Hideki Noda invented *Sandaime Richard*, loosely based on the Bard's history play. Noda's play, first performed in 1990, is a witty satire on power that parallels the Wars of the Roses in England and the intrigue in the *ikebana* (flower arrangement) clan in Japan. Shakespeare is put on trial for falsifying history and defaming Sandaime Richard, the *iemoto* (grand master) of the *ikebana*. Shakespeare is also prosecuted by Maachan of Venice, who has been defamed by Shakespeare's writing and tries to exact revenge on the Bard.

Ong Keng Sen, well-known for his cutting-edge productions of Shakespeare plays, has actively contributed to the transglobalisation of contemporary Asian performing arts. He boldly reworks and directs Noda's play, which appears to be an iconoclastic farce but still represents Noda's firm belief in the freedom of expression, imagination and creativity, expressed in Noda's own ingenious way. In Ong's multilingual and intercultural collaborative version for the 2016 International Festival in April-May in Shizuoka and in September in Singapore, he juxtaposes Asian traditional performance forms, with eight members and cross-gender casting: Nakamura Kazutaro (a Kabuki actor skilled in *onnagata* [female impersonator], Richard III/Richard), Shigeyama Doji (a *kyogen* [Noh comic interlude] actor, Shakespeare/George), Janice Koh (Singaporean, Maachan/Shylock), Jajang C Noer (Indonesian, Shakespeare's Mother/ Iemoto's Wife), I Kadek Budi Setiawan (a Balinese shadow-play performer, Chabozu/Puppets), Emoto Junko (a contemporary dramatist of Kegawazoku, Chiropractor/Truth), Takii Miki (a performer of the SPAC, Shakespeare's Wife/Anne), Kuze Seika (a former star of the all-female Takarazuka revue company skilled in *otokoyaku* [male roles], Judge/ Shakespeare's Father/Iemoto/Keepsake) (*Sandaime Richard*, programme, 5). In his productions of Shakespeare's adaptations,[1] Ong tackles cross-gender casting while emphasising Old Asia and New Asia. In this production, Ong successfully subverts the fixed gender dualism by casting the Kabuki *onnagata* and the Takarazuka *otokoyaku*, who both subvert fixed gender roles in their respective style.

As I pointed out in Chapter 6, Ong's boldly multicultural, hybrid and deconstructed works have been criticised by those who do not fully understand his artistic and political principles. It is no wonder that some reviewers have criticised *Sandaime Richard* for its hybridity and discord. While Ong is aware of the French philosopher Jean-Luc Nancy's approach to *mondialisation*—an authentic world-forming—as resistance to globalisation and the uniformity and injustice to which it leads,[2] Ong does not intend to merge or fuse cultures and traditions but rather hopes to sustain differences and discord. He has never tried to smooth out all the rough edges of cultures, which, in my view, is likely to produce "real" intercultural or transcultural theatre. Ong has not employed a fixed singular style or method; instead, while appreciating the comparatively recent revival of Deleuze and Guattari in American academic circles, he thinks that one of his strongest drives is to remain affected by people he works with and to find ways to affect them. Ong is different from Western auteur directors. Employing a range of techniques to create *Sandaime Richard*, he adopts a collective method in which he allows the performers to influence the creative process. Although it might be at times risky and incoherent, his flexible method can contribute to collaborative artistic innovation and a fair world-forming by accommodating diversity. In her recent article on Ong's "diasporic performance," Alexa Huang suggests that audiences and critics have often misunderstood Ong due to their cultural essentialism and rightly states that, given the "Disneyfication of Asian cultures, the effect of Ong's amalgamated styles is the creation of a counterbalance of the mindless synthesis of cultures at international festivals" ("Global Diasporas" 1216). Obviously, *Sandaime Richard* is no perfect synthesis, as it shows the collision of a diversity of performing styles in Asia at their cultural interfaces. Our senses are almost paralysed by this bold and flamboyant production of an extremely complicated and multi-layered play and by the overflow or Disneyfication of electric music, projected images of technicoloured flowers and other analogue and digital scenography. That said, I would like to insist that the production should be appreciated in a broad critical context. A diversity of Japanese traditional and contemporary performing forms, ranging from *kyogen*, Kabuki and Takarazuka to contemporary little theatre are blended. Although they have been, directly or not, influenced by one another, they maintain their rough edges in terms of artistic philosophy, acting style and speed. Ong's production of *Sandaime Richard* offers a present-day reality and the challenge of Japanese theatre arts.

Sandaime Richard begins and ends with a Balinese shadow play with gamelan music, using puppets especially made and decorated for this show. Its ending is especially effective by projecting the world tree on a translucent screen, which symbolises heaven in the style of a Balinese shadow play. It is the greatest moment of cognitive impact on the audience, who are affected by its sublime beauty, intensity and expansion. Ironically, the sublime moment of this intercultural or diasporic performance lies in its ending, which is a brilliant addition. The world tree, also called the cosmic tree or the tree of life (*kayon* or *kayonan*) as the *axis mundi*, is a widespread motif in many myths and folktales in Asia, and this symbol embraces all the confusion and cultural rough edges exposed on the stage, making us aware of the transglobal value of theatrical imagination and world-forming creativity.[3]

Notes

Part I Intercultural and Multilingual Performance
Chapter 1 This Is, and Is Not, Shakespeare: A Japanese-Korean Transformation of *Othello*

1. There appears to be an affinity between global Shakespeare and world literature. Damrosch (2003) writes: "English Literature is now as much a global as a national phenomenon, and both its language and its thematic resources can be multiply exploited, at once from inside and from outside, as writers triangulate among the local, the international, and the personal landscapes of their worlds" (230).
2. A linguistic problem should be noted. Global Shakespeare facilitates local Shakespeares, but it is hard for non-locals to understand and discuss them, unless they are performed in English as a global language or with English subtitles.
3. The following section is based on part of the extensively revised version of my "*Othello* in the Japanese *Mugen* Noh Style."
4. A useful chronology of "Shakespeare in Hollywood, Asia and Cyberspace" is provided by Alexander Huang (*Chinese Shakespeares* 265-74).
5. Singleton (2009) examines two Korean productions of Shakespeare plays that were performed at the Barbican Centre in London in 2006: Mokwha Theatre Company's *Romeo and Juliet,* directed by Oh Tae-suk, and Yohangza Theatre Company's *A Midsummer Night's Dream,* directed by Yang Jung-ung. Singleton concludes: "What we were witnessing then in London was glocalisation of an international brand (i.e., Shakespeare) in performance. This is hugely significant for the future of the *inter*cultural, as it is *intra*cultural experience that challenges national ownership of any culture, Asian or European.... These productions manifest a 'pursuit of otherness for the investigation of self'.... That self can be national or international, local or global, and is a self that is

redolent of a desire for casting an eye intraculturally to heritage, pastness and ancient tradition to illuminate the contemporary experience of being in the world" (196-97).

6. When Shakespeare's work is the main subject of a chapter, its lines are quoted from a separate textbook of the *Arden Shakespeare*, 3rd series: in this chapter, for example, *Othello*, edited by E. A. J. Honigmann. Otherwise, his lines are usually quoted throughout this book from *The Arden Shakespeare Complete Works*.

Chapter 2 Performing Shakespeare after the 11 March 2011 Disaster: Yamanote Jijosha's *The Tempest*

1. The title of the song "Iihi Tabidachi," written and composed by Shinji Tanimura in 1978, literally means "a nice day for departure." It was translated into English and made into a hit entitled "Days That Used to Be," written by Clive Scott and Des Dyer and sung by the Nolans, an Irish-born British female group, in the 1980s.
2. The English-language version of "Days That Used to Be" represents the sentimental atmosphere and overall mood of the original Japanese song.

Chapter 3 The Last Shakespeare Plays Directed by Yukio Ninagawa: Possessed by the Power of Theatre

1. Alexa Huang discusses "three interconnected channels" for the emergence of boomerang Shakespeare in Britain. "The first channel is intercultural borrowing" against the background of the Paris intercultural movement in the 1980s (1096). A second channel is "subtitled touring productions" (1097). There are several serious issues in the reception history of boomerang Shakespeare: for example, Western stereotypical expectations of non-Western directions with their special focus on their traditional visual and sensory dimensions. The third channel is "coproductions between UK and foreign artists or companies, a growth area of theatre practice" (1098). There are other serious political faces of boomerang Shakespeare, since obviously it is an "integral part of Britain's campaign for soft power and self-identity in a

postcolonial global age" (1100).

2. As many references to Ninagawa's work are already available (e.g., Hamana, *Connecting Cultures* 25-36, 87-102; Alexander Huang, "Yukio Ninagawa"; Kawai, "Ninagawa Yukio"), I discussed his eighth *Hamlet* production from the new perspective of his idea of the power of theatre (Hamana, "*Hamlet* (2015)").

3. Uchida (47) writes that when Ninagawa directed the tango dance scene in *Richard II*, he was inspired by Ken Russell's film *Valentino* (1977), which includes a homoerotic tango scene between two men, Rudolph Valentino (Rudolph Nureyev) and a young man.

Chapter 4 Multilingual Performances of Shakespeare Worldwide: Multilingual *King Lear*, Directed by Tadashi Suzuki

1. Martin-Jones et al. (10). The book quoted several times in the paragraph is *Disinventing and Reconstituting Languages*, edited by S. Makoni and A. Pennycook (Multilingual Matters, 2007).

2. Canagarajah, however, proposed the term "translingual" for a different paradigm. Canagarajah criticised "the term *multilingual*" especially because it "doesn't accommodate the dynamic interactions between languages and communities envisioned by translingual" (*Literacy as Translingual Practice* 7). Part II of the present volume explores the challenges and possibilities of translingual performance of Shakespeare's plays.

3. See Hamana, "A Report on Globe to Globe 2012," and Bennett and Carson, esp. 1-11.

4. Hutcheon correctly notes that "in the working of the human imagination, adaptation is the norm, not the exception" (177). See also Malcolm and Marshall 1-10.

5. SCOT homepage, 8 Aug. 2013. My English translation and italics. Some multinational theatre companies, such as Peter Brook's International Centre for Theatre Research in Paris, are well known for their multilingual performances. In Europe, multilingual performers seem to pursue transculturalism or cosmopolitanism, while in colonised nations they seem to strive for postcolonialism. In Japan, we can find several multilingual theatre companies:

for example, Utsubo has performed multilingual plays with casts made up of Japanese and foreign students. Yudai Kamisato, a Peru-born and prize-winning playwright, among others, is highly promising.
6. See Allain, esp. 191; Carruthers ch. 10; Minami et al. 121-32; Sellers-Young 406-409; Suzuki, *Culture is the Body* 104-16; Suzuki, "Interview"; Suzuki, *What is Theatre?* 94-97.
7. Regarding the details, see Carruthers and Takahashi 98-99.
8. See Takahashi, "Suzuki's Shakespeare (II)" and Carruthers and Takahashi.
9. See Yong, "Shakespeare Here and There" 191-99.
10. See Peterson, esp. 64, and Ren.
11. Significantly, however, Ong Keng Sen states that he has not been satisfied with paralleling languages and traditional expressions since he directed *Lear* and that in directing *Desdemona*, he became more process-oriented. See Greham, 181-84 notes. Ong's *Lear Dreaming*, performed at the Singapore Arts Festival in May–June 2012, appears to experiment with translingualism while reducing verbal elements to a minimum and exploiting nonverbal and semiotic resources like music, dance and laser beams. See Chapter 6 of this volume.
12. Suzuki, *Collected Works* 15-20. The act, scene and line numbers shown in the following brackets are from this text.
13. See Rozbicki and Ndege 217.

Part II Translingual Performance
Chapter 6 *Lear Dreaming*, Directed by Ong Keng Sen

1. Kishida's original version is available in Japanese (57-146).
2. Ong's commitment to intercultural and multilingual productions is also closely related to the multilingual and multicultural reality of Singapore (Peterson, *Theatre and the Politics of Culture* 203-18; Russell and Cohn 5-32).
3. Ong directed *Richard III* as *Sandaime Richard*, adapted by Hideki Noda, in Shizuoka, Japan, in May 2016; it was his newest intercultural work of one of Shakespeare's plays. See Appendix.
4. The making of transnational theatre or intercultural theatre is inseparable from the question of translation. Neill rightly states that translation "is never

innocent, and its motives are usually mixed, but only through its uncertain operations, Shakespeare suggests, can human beings stretch their fragile pontoons into the unknown" (417).

5. English quotations form *Lear Dreaming* are based on the text in the Asian Shakespeare Intercultural Archive (A|S|I|A). Both the script and video were donated to A|S|I|A by TheatreWorks, and the English translation was edited by Li Lan Yong. The video consists of thirteen scenes; speeches and lyrics are shown without their line numbers.

6. While exploring new forms for performative Shakespeare criticism and considering the affective force of a Shakespeare play in performance, Conkie argues that five affective spheres—actor affect, character affect, narrative affect, personal affect and performative affect—result in a cumulative performance affect (112). When we focus on the affective force in a Shakespeare play, adapted or not, this analytical form might work or at least seems worth attempting.

7. Pavis quotes from the following two books: Margaret Croyden, editor, *Conversations with Peter Brook* (Faber, 2004) and Jean-François Lyotard, *Des dispositifs pulsionnels* (Union Generale d'Editions, 1973).

8. In his prize-winning translation of Zeami, Tom Hare translates the same chapter or article into "On Binding the Many Arts with a Single Intent" and the same passage as follows: "It is a frame of mind in which you maintain your intent and do not loosen your concentration.... The internal excitement diffuses outward and creates interest" (115). Harc's version is largely faithful to Zeami's original note and is therefore at times ambiguous or opaque.

9. Regarding Ong's direction of *Sandaime Richard* (2016), see Appendix.

Chapter 7 *Safaring the Night: A Midsummer Night's Dream* Updated

1. The title of this work is obviously ungrammatical first because "safari" is an intransitive verb and second because its progressive form is "safariing." However, its unusual form seems to fit perfectly here, evoking the sight of touring the special night when the two AI enterprises are going to be integrated into an unknown world or in pseudo-virtual reality, with a smartphone and Apple's Safari browser.

2. See Socrates, which examines 16 definitions chronologically and asks us for the 17th definition before finally pointing out, "we really do not know what the singularity is (or will be)." Despite our ignorance, it is still of vital importance to consider the relation between technology and humankind, just as Ito is trying to do in his play.
3. *Safaring the Night*, "Programme," my translation with some additions.
4. In her paper on *A Midsummer Night's Dream*, focusing on the keyword "shadows," which refers to both an actor and a character, Amy Cook writes: "When the spectator attends to the actor onstage, a character is created as a result, something that categorises the stimuli, generates predictions and affords reactions. This happens during any performance … but Shakespeare turns it into a coup de théâtre by creating characters that point from themselves to their roles" (113). Transforming several main shadows into invisible entities or machines, which generate action and afford reactions, *Safaring the Night* can be another version of a coup de théâtre.
5. See Sakurai. In this connection, consider the 2017 science fiction film *Blade Runner 2049*, a sequel to the 1982 film *Blade Runner*, dealing with a war between humans and replicants.
6. Shakespeare, *A Midsummer Night's Dream*, edited by Harold F. Brooks and collected in *The Arden Shakespeare Complete Works* 887-910; Preface, 887. Although Chaudhuri, the editor of the Arden 3rd series, summarises the recent study of sources and analogues of the play (44-71), Brooks's summary of the sources in the Arden 2nd series remains valid.
7. In this connection, I would like to mention in particular Shakespeare's changing language in the digital world. In 2013, the Royal Shakespeare Company, partnering with Google Creative Lab, mounted a production of *A Midsummer Night's Dream* that combined digital and live events. Quoting Tom Uglow of the Lab, Christie Carson and Peter Kirwan say that his "suggestion that social media habits involve a form of immersion is telling" (238). The semiotic resources of Shakespeare's performance, as well as ecological affordances, have been changing and, despite possible criticism, adapting themselves to today's audience.
8. The distance between humans and AIs (humanoids) has closed, and humanoids

may indeed have a type of human mind in the future. In his first science fiction novel, *Hito wa Android ni naru tameni* (*For Humans to Become Androids*), Hiroshi Ishiguro, a world-renowned humanoid researcher and professor at Osaka University, explores the relationship between humans and humanoids in the future, once the brain-uploading technology of copying human brains to machines becomes available (Ishiguro and Iida 249-94).

9. I restrict myself mainly to comparing *Safaring the Night* to science fiction films here because I will discuss Shakespeare plays in immersive theatre in a separate paper.

Appendix: Performance Review: *Sandaime Richard,* written by Hideki Noda and directed by Ong Keng Sen.

1. See Mika Eglinton, "Performing 'Women' in 'Asia,' Ong Keng Sen's Shakespeare Trilogy: *Lear, Desdemona*, and *Search: Hamlet*," *Theatre and Film Studies 2011*, vol.5. Waseda University, 2012, pp. 95-121.
2. See Nancy 27-28.
3. I wondered if the use of electric music and projected images in this production might be excessive; however, it may have been appropriate for a non-Japanese audience, especially during the September 2016 performance in Singapore (see Nanda).

Works Cited

Akishima, Yuriko. *Yukio Ninagawa and William Shakespeare*. Kadokawa, 2015.
Allain, Paul. *The Theatre Practice of Tadashi Suzuki: A Critical Study with DVD Examples*. Bloomsbury, 2002.
Asai, Nobumichi. "Real-Time Face Generator/kagami." *Vimeo*. https://vimeo.com/186075392. Accessed 21 Aug. 2018.
Bakker, Peter, and Yaron Matras, editors. *Contact Languages: A Comprehensive Guide*. Walter de Gruyter, 2013.
Bauman, Zygmunt. *Modernity and Ambivalence*. Polity Press, 1993.
Bennett, Susan. *Theatre Audiences: A Theory of Production and Reception*. 2nd ed., Routledge, 1997.
Bennett, Susan, and Christie Carson, editors. *Shakespeare Beyond English: A Global Experiment*. Cambridge UP, 2013.
Bharucha, Rustom. *The Politics of Cultural Practice: Thinking Through Theatre in an Age of Globalisation*. Wesleyan University Press, 2000.
Billington, Michael. "Yukio Ninagawa Obituary." *The Guardian*, 16 May 2016. https://www.theguardian.com/stage/2016/may/16/yukio-ninagawa-obituary. Accessed 21 Aug. 2018.
Blank, Paula. *Broken English: Dialects and the Politics of Language in Renaissance Writings*. Routledge, 1996.
Braunmuller, Albert. R. "Macbeth, Three Influential Late Twentieth-Century Productions: Kurosawa, Polanski, Ninagawa." *The Cambridge Guide to the Worlds of Shakespeare*, edited by Bruce Smith, Cambridge UP, 2016. 2 vols., vol. 2, pp. 1604-07.
Burke, Peter. *Languages and Communities in Early Modern Europe (The Wiles Lectures)*. Cambridge UP, 2004.
Burnett, Mark Thornton, and Ramona Wray, editors. *Shakespeare and Ireland: History, Politics, Culture*. Macmillan, 1997.
Canagarajah, A. Suresh, editor. *Literacy as Translingual Practice Between Communities and Classrooms*. Routledge, 2013.

———. *Translingual Practice: Global Englishes and Cosmopolitan Relations*. Routledge, 2012.

Carlson, Marvin. *Speaking in Tongues: Languages at Play in the Theatre*. U of Michigan P, 2009.

Carruthers, Ian. *The Theatre of Suzuki Tadashi*. Cambridge UP, 2004.

Carruthers, Ian, and Yasunari Takahashi. "Fooling with Lear: A Performance History of Suzuki Tadashi's *King Lear* (1984–2006)." *Re-Playing Shakespeare in Asia*, edited by Poonam Trivedi and Ryuta Minami, Routledge, 2010, pp. 97-118.

Carson, Christie and Peter Kirwan, editors. *Shakespeare and the Digital World*. Cambridge UP, 2014

Cefalu, Paul. *Tragic Cognition in Shakespeare's 'Othello': Beyond the Neural Sublime*. Bloomsbury, 2015.

Collins, Jane, and Andrew Nisbet, editors. *Theatre and Performance Design: A Reader in Scenography*. Routledge, 2010.

Conkie, Rob. *Writing Performative Shakespeares: New Forms for Performance Criticism*. Cambridge UP, 2016.

Cook, Amy. "King of Shadows: Early Modern Characters and Actors." *Shakespeare and Consciousness*, edited by Paul Budra and Clifford Werier, Palgrave, 2016, pp. 99-118.

Croyden, Margaret, editor. *Conversations with Peter Brook*. Faber, 2004.

Crunell-Vanrigh, Anny. "'Fause Frenche Enough': Kate's French in Shakespeare's *Henry V*." *Multilingualism in the Drama of Shakespeare and his Contemporaries*, special issue of *English Text Construction*, vol. 6, no. 1, 2013, pp. 60-88.

Damrosch, David. *What Is World Literature?* Princeton UP, 2003.

Delabastita, Dirk, and Ton Hoenselaars. "'If but as well I Other Accents Borrow, That Can my Speech Diffuse': Multilingual Perspectives on English Renaissance Drama." *Multilingualism in the Drama of Shakespeare and his Contemporaries*, special issue of *English Text Construction*, vol. 6, no. 1, 2013, pp. 1-16.

Derrida, Jacques. "Des tours de Babel." *Psyche: Inventions of the Other*, edited by Peggy Kamuf and Elizabeth Rottenberg, and translated by Joseph F. Graham, Stanford UP, 2007, vol. 1, pp. 191-225.

Dionne, Craig and Parmita Kapadia, editors. *Native Shakespeares: Indigenous Appropriations on a Global Stage*. Ashgate, 2008.

Dotov, Dobromir G. et al. "Understanding Affordances: History and Contemporary Development of Gibson's Central Concept." *Avant: the Journal of the Philosophical-Interdisciplinary Vanguard*, vol. 3, no.2, 2012, pp. 28-39.

Dymkowski, Christine, editor. *Shakespeare in Production: The Tempest*. Cambridge UP, 2000.

Edmondson, Paul et al., editors. *A Year of Shakespeare: Re-living the World Shakespeare Festival*. Bloomsbury, 2013.

Eglinton, Mika. "Performing Constraint through *Yojohan*: Yamanote Jijosha's *Titus Andronicus*." *Shakespeare Studies*, vol. 49, 2012, pp. 12-28.

Gaines, Barry. "Monumental Japanese Production of Shakespeare's *Richard II* Opens Romanian Festival." 30 April 2016. https://barryreviews.wordpress.com/2016/04/30/monumental-japanese-production-of-shakespeares-richard-ii-opens-romanian-festival/. Accessed 21 Aug. 2018.

Gelderen, Elly van. *A History of the English Language*. John Benjamins, 2006.

Gibson, James J. *The Ecological Approach to Visual Perception*. Houghton Mifflin, 1979.

Gikandi, Simon. "Editor's Column—Provincializing English." *PMLA*, vol. 129, no.1, 2014, pp. 7-17.

Greenblatt, Stephen. *Marvelous Possessions: The Wonder of the New World*. Oxford UP, 1991.

Greham, Helena. *Performance, Ethics and Spectatorship in a Global Age*. Palgrave Macmillan, 2009.

Hamana, Emi. *Connecting Cultures: From Shakespeare to Contemporary Asian Theatre* (in Japanese). Tsukuba UP, 2012.

———. "Contemporary Japanese Responses to Shakespeare: Problems and Possibilities." *Theatre International: East-West Perspectives on Theatre: Essays on the Theory and Praxis of World Drama*, edited by Tapu Biswas et al., vol. V. Shakespeare Special Number. Avantgarde Press, 2012, pp. 11-25.

———. "*Hamlet* (2015), Directed by Yukio Ninagawa: Possessed by the Power of Theatre." *Shakespeare: His Infinite Variety*, edited by Krystyna Kujawińska Courtney and Grzegorz Zinkiewicz, Lodz UP, 2017, pp. 133-44.

———. "*Othello* in the Japanese *Mugen* Noh Style with Elements of Korean Shamanism." *Studies in Literature and Linguistics* (Tsukuba University), vol. 59, 2011, pp. 75-91.

———. "A Report on Globe to Globe 2012: Shakespeare's 37 Plays in 37 Languages." *Studies in Foreign Languages* (Language Centre, Tsukuba University), vol.35, 2013, pp. 123-35.

Heijes, Coen. "The Multiple Faces of a Multicultural Society. Theatre Review. *The Tempest*. Dir. Janice Honeyman. The Baxter Theatre Centre (Cape Town, South Africa) and the Royal Shakespeare Company (Stratford-upon-Avon, United Kingdom)." *Multicultural Shakespeare: Translation, Appropriation and Performance*, vol. 8, 2012, pp. 139-42.

Hodgdon, Barbara. "Afterword: Do Dead Playwrights Have Rights?" *World-Wide Shakespeares: Local Appropriations in Film and Performance*, edited by Sonia Massai, Routledge, 2005, pp. 158-59.

Hoenselaars, Ton. "International Encounters." *The Cambridge Guide to the Worlds of Shakespeare*, edited by Bruce Smith, Cambridge UP, 2016. 2 vols., vol. 2, pp. 1033-46.

———. "In the Shadow of St. Paul's: Linguistic Confusion in English Renaissance Drama." *English Literature and the Other Languages*, edited by Ton Hoenselaars and Marius Buning, Rodopi, 1999, pp. 27-40.

———, editor. *Shakespeare and the Language of Translation*. Bloomsbury, 2004.

———. "Translation Futures: Shakespearians and the Foreign Text." *Shakespeare Survey 62: Close Encounters with Shakespeare's Text*, edited by Peter Holland, Cambridge UP, 2009, pp. 273-82.

Hoenselaars, Ton, and Marius Buning, editors. *English Literature and the Other Languages*. Rodopi, 1999.

Hsy, Jonathan. *Trading Tongues: Merchants, Multilingualism, and Medieval Literature*. Ohio State UP, 2013.

Huang, Alexa. "Boomerang Shakespeare: Foreign Shakespeare in Britain." *The Cambridge Guide to the Worlds of Shakespeare*, edited by Bruce Smith, Cambridge UP, 2016. 2 vols., vol. 2, pp. 1094-1101.

———. "Global Diasporas as Reflected in The Work of Keng Sen Ong." *The Cambridge Guide to the Worlds of Shakespeare*, edited by Bruce Smith, Cambridge UP, 2016. 2 vols., vol. 2, pp. 1212-19.

Huang, Alexander C. Y. *Chinese Shakespeares: Two Centuries of Cultural Exchange*. Colombia UP, 2009.

———. "Yukio Ninagawa." *Brook, Hall, Ninagawa, Lepage. Great Shakespeareans*, vol. XVIII, edited by Peter Holland, Bloomsbury, 2013, pp. 79-112.

Hutcheon, Linda. *A Theory of Adaptation*. 2nd ed., Routledge, 2013.

Institute for the Exploration of Virtual Realities (i.e.VR). *A Midsummer Night's Dream*. http://www2.ku.edu/~ievr/midsummer/. Accessed 21 Aug. 2018.

Ishiguro, Hiroshi and Ichishi Iida. *Hito ha Android ni naru tameni (For Humans to Become Androids)*. Chikuma Shobo, 2017.

Ito, Yasuro. "Interview on *Safaring the Night*." https://www.cinra.net/column/201703-safaringthenight. Accessed on 21 Aug. 2018.

———. "A Short Commentary on *Safaring the Night*." Ito's blog, *Hitomoncyaku-Kaigi*, 7 March 2017. https://ameblo.jp/yasuroito/day-20170307.html. Accessed 21 Aug. 2018.

Ivic, Christopher. "'Bastard Normans, Norman Bastards': Anomalous Identities in *The Life of Henry the Fift*." *Shakespeare and Wales: From the Marches to the Assembly*, edited by Willy Maley and Philip Schwyzer, Ashgate, 2010, pp. 75-90.

Kawachi, Yoshiko. "Shakespeare's History Plays in Japan." *Multicultural Shakespeare: Translation, Appropriation and Performance*, vol. 3, 2006, pp. 45-55.

Kawai, Shoichiro. "Ninagawa Yukio." *The Routledge Companion to Directors' Shakespeare*, edited by John Russell Brown, Routledge, 2008, pp. 269-83.

———. "The Significance of Producing *Richard II* for the Saitama Shakespeare Series." *Higeki Kigeki*, no.780, May 2016, pp. 62-64.

Kellman, Steven G., editor. *Switching Languages: Translingual Writers Reflect on Their Craft*. U of Nebraska P, 2003.

———. *The Translingual Imagination*. U of Nebraska P, 2000.

Kemp, Rick. *Embodied Acting: What Neuroscience Tells Us About Performance*. Routledge, 2012.

Kennedy, Dennis, editor. *The Oxford Encyclopedia of Theatre and Performance*. 2 vols., Oxford UP, 2003.

Kennedy, Dennis and Li Lan Yong, editors. *Shakespeare in Asia: Contemporary Performance*. Cambridge UP, 2010.

Kermode, Lloyd Edward. *Aliens and Englishness in Elizabethan Drama*. Cambridge UP, 2009.

Kerrigan, John. *Archipelagic English: Literature, History, and Politics 1603-1707.* Oxford UP, 2008.

Kibbee, Douglas A. *For to Speke Frenche Trewely: The French Language in England, 1000–1600: Its Status, Description and Instruction.* John Benjamins, 1991.

Kishi, Tetsuo and Graham Bradshaw. *Shakespeare in Japan.* Continuum, 2005.

Kishida, Rio. *Lear. Collected Works of Rio Kishida*, vol. 3. Jiritsu Shobo, 2004.

Koh, Boon Pin. *From Identity to Mondialisation: TheatreWorks 25.* Editions Didier Millet, 2013.

Krzyzanowski, Jerzy R. "Witold Gombrowicz". *Encyclopædia Britannica.* 2015. https://www.britannica.com/biography/Witold-Gombrowicz. Accessed 21 Aug. 2018.

Lee, Hyon-u et al. *Glocalizing Shakespeare in Korea and Beyond.* Dongin Publishing, 2009.

Lee, Youn-taek. Interview, 30 September 2008. https://festival-tokyo.jp/09sp/press/Othello-pdf. Accessed 21 Aug. 2018.

———. Post-performance talk, 28 February 2009.

Lennon, Brian. *In Babel's Shadow: Multilingual Literatures, Monolingual States.* U of Minnesota P, 2010.

Luu, Lien Bich. *Immigrants and the Industries of London, 1500-1700.* Ashgate, 2005.

Lynne, Raphael. *Shakespeare, Rhetoric and Cognition.* Cambridge UP, 2011.

McConachie, Bruce. *Engaging Audiences: A Cognitive Approach to Spectating in the Theatre.* Palgrave, 2008.

McConachie, Bruce, and F. Elizabeth Hart, editors. *Performance and Cognition: Theatre Studies and the Cognitive Turn.* Routledge, 2006.

McKinney, Joslin, and Philip Butterworth. *The Cambridge Introduction to Scenography.* Cambridge UP, 2009.

Mahasarinand, Pawit. "Meeting, Not Merging." *The Nation*, 29 Jul. 2012. http://www.nationmultimedia.com/life/Meeting-not-merging-30186461.html. Accessed 21 Aug. 2018.

Malcolm, Gabrielle and Keli Marshall. *Locating Shakespeare in the Twenty-First Century.* Cambridge Scholars Publishing, 2012.

Maniutiu, Mihai. "Magic in Theatre." *Performance Studies: Key Words, Concepts and Theories*, edited by Bryan Reynolds, and translated by Cipriana Petre,

Palgrave, 2014, pp. 244-47.
Martin-Jones et al., editors. *The Routledge Handbook of Multilingualism*. Routledge, 2012.
Minami, Ryuta, Ian Carruthers, and John Gilles, editors. *Performing Shakespeare in Japan*. Cambridge UP, 2001.
Montgomery, Marianne. *Europe's Languages on England's Stages, 1590-1620*. Ashgate, 2012.
Motohashi, Tetsuya. "An Unawakened Nightmare, the Repetition of a Written Language, or the Bermuda Triangle: A Review of Yamanote Jijosha's *The Tempest*," translated by Emi Hamana, *Theatre Arts*, 31 Jan. 2015. http://theatrearts.aict-iatc.jp/201501/2510/. Accessed 21 Aug. 2018.
Nancy, Jean-Luc. *The Creation of the World or Globalisation*. Translated by François Raffoul and David Pettigrew, State U of New York P, 2007.
Nanda, Akshita. "Madcap Visual Comedy on Shakespeare." *The Straight Times*, 10 Sep. 2016. https://www.straitstimes.com/lifestyle/arts/madcap-visual-comedy-on-shakespeare. Accessed 21 Aug, 2018.
National Theatre Wales website. http://www.nationaltheatrewales.org/waleslab-japan/underground-airport. Accessed 21 Aug. 2018.
Neill, Michael. *Putting History to the Question: Power, Politics, and Society in English Renaissance Drama*. Columbia UP, 1993.
Nicholl, Charles. *The Lodger: Shakespeare on Silver Street*. Penguin, 2008.
Ninagawa, Yukio. "Documentary: Yukio Ninagawa's Challenge." NHK BS Premium. 4 June 2016.
———. *Engeki no Chikara* (*The Power of Theatre*). Nihon Keizai Shimbun Press, 2013.
———. "Special Interview with Yukio Ninagawa Theatre Director." NHK 1. 28 May 2016.
Ninagawa, Yukio, and Hiroshi Hasebe. *Engijutsu* (The Art of Direction). Chikuma Shobo, 2012.
NINAGAWA Macbeth. "Programme." Hori Production Inc., 2015.
Nolans, The. *Best of Best*. Sony Music Direct (Japan) Inc. 2007.
Ong, Keng Sen. "Director's Notes on *Lear Dreaming*." http://www.theatreworks.org.sg/international/leardreaming/notes.html. Accessed 21 Aug. 2018.
———. *Lear Dreaming*, directed by Ong. Video(s) of Ong's productions can be

accessed at: http://www.a-s-i-a-web.org.

———. "Mondialisation or World Forming in The Flying Circus Project." Transcultural. Transnational. Transformation. Seeing, Writing and Reading Performance Across Cultures 2011. Australasian Association for Theatre, Drama and Performance Studies Conference 2011. Keynote Address. https://www.adsa.edu.au/db_uploads/ADSA_2011_program_and_abstracts.pdf, 13-4. Accessed 21 Aug. 2018.

Orkin, Martin. *Local Shakespeares: Proximations and Power*. Routledge, 2005.

OED Online. Accessed 25 Aug. 2016.

Parker, Patricia. "6. Uncertain Unions: Welsh Leeks in *Henry V*." *British Identities and English Renaissance Literature*, edited by J. David Baker and Willy Maley, Cambridge UP, 2002, pp. 81-99.

Pavis, Patrice. *The Routledge Dictionary of Performance and Contemporary Theatre*. Translated by Andrew Brown. Routledge, 2016.

Peterson, William. "Being Affected: An Interview with Ong Ken Sen of TheatreWorks Singapore in Conversation with William Peterson." *Theatre and Adaptation: Return, Rewrite, Repeat*, edited by Margherita Laera, Bloomsbury, 2014, pp. 165-179.

———. *Theatre and the Politics of Culture in Contemporary Singapore*. Wesleyan UP, 2001.

Porter, Lisa, with Samantha Watson. "Ong Keng Sen's *Lear Dreaming*: Humanity and Power in Process." *Theatre Forum*, no. 43, 2013, pp. 80-90.

Pratt, M. L. "Arts of the Contact Zone." *Profession*, pp. 33-40. https://www.jstor.org/stable/25595469?seq=1#page_scan_tab_contents. Accessed 21 Aug. 2018.

Project Hush. http://www.papertrail.org.uk/?project=project-hush. Accessed 21 Aug. 2018.

Ren, Quah Sy. "Performing Multilingualism in Singapore." *Between Tongues: Translation, and/of/in Performance in Asia*, edited by Jennifer Lindsay, Singapore UP, 2006, 88-103.

Reynolds, Bryan, editor. *Performance Studies: Key Words, Concepts and Theories*. Palgrave, 2014.

Reynolds, Bryan, and Ayanna Thompson. "Inspriteful Ariels: Transversal Tempests." *Performing Transversally: Reimaging Shakespeare and the Critical Future*, edited by Bryan Reynolds, Palgrave, 2003, pp. 189-214.

Rozbicki, Michael Jan, and George O. Ndege, editors. *Cross-Cultural History and the Domestication of Otherness*. Palgrave Macmillan, 2012.

Russell, Jesse, and Ronald Cohn. *Ong Keng Sen*. Lennex, 2012.

Saenger, Michael. "Interlinguicity and *The Alchemist*." *English Literary Construction*, vol. 6, no.1. 2013, pp. 176-200.

———. *Shakespeare and the French Borders of English*. Palgrave, 2013.

Safaring the Night. Programme. 2017.

Saitama Arts Theatre. Homepage. http://www.saf.or.jp/en/venues/. Accessed 21 Aug. 2018.

Sakurai, Hiromitsu. "Performance Review of *Safaring the Night*." http://enterstage.jp/news/2017/03/006677.html. Accessed 21 Aug. 2018.

Sandaime Richard. Programme. Shizuoka Performing Arts Center, 2016.

Sanders, Julie. *Adaptation and Appropriation*. Routledge, 2006.

Sasayama, Takashi et al., editors. *Shakespeare and the Japanese Stage*. Cambridge UP, 1998.

Sellers-Young, Barbara. "The One Pointed Mind: Japanese Influence on Contemporary Actor Training in the United States." *Japanese Theatre and the International Stage,* edited by Stanca Scholz-Cionca and Samuel L. Leiter, Brill, 2001, pp. 397-409.

Shakespeare, William. *The Arden Shakespeare Complete Works,* edited by Richard Proudfoot, Ann Thompson and David Scott Kastan, Thomas Nelson, 1998.

———. *Hamlet*. The Arden Shakespeare, 3rd series, edited by Harold Jenkins, Methuen, 1982, and Thomas Nelson and Sons, 1997.

———. *King Henry V*. The Arden Shakespeare, 3rd series, edited by T. W. Craik, Routledge, 1995.

———. *King Lear*. The Arden Shakespeare, 3rd series, edited by R. A. Foakes, Thomas Nelson, 1997.

———. *Macbeth*. The Arden Shakespeare, 3rd series, edited by Sandra Clark and Pamela Mason, Bloomsbury, 2015.

———. *A Midsummer Night's Dream*. The Arden Shakespeare, 3rd series, edited by Sukanta Chaudhuri, Bloomsbury, 2017.

———. *Othello*. The Arden Shakespeare, 3rd series, edited by F. A. J. Honigmann,

Thomas and Nelson, 1999.

———. *Richard II*. The Arden Shakespeare, 3rd series, edited by Charles R. Forker, Bloomsbury, 2002.

———. *The Tempest*. The Arden Shakespeare, 3rd series, edited by Virginia Mason Vaughan and Alden T. Vaughan. Thomas Nelson, 1999.

Shepherd, Simon and Mick Wallis. *Drama/Theatre/Performance*. Routledge, 2004.

Singleton, Brian. "Interculturalism." *The Oxford Encyclopedia of Theatre and Performance*, edited by Dennis Kennedy. Oxford UP, 2003, vol.1, pp. 628-30.

———. "Intercultural Shakespeare from Intracultural Sources: Two Korean Performances." *Glocalizing Shakespeare in Korea and Beyond*, written by Lee Hyon-u et al., Dongin Publishing, 2009, pp. 179-98.

Smith, Bruce R., general editor. *The Cambridge Guide to the Worlds of Shakespeare*. 2 vols. Cambridge UP, 2016.

Socrates. "17 Definitions of the Technological Singularity." https://www.singularityweblog.com/17-definitions-of-the-technological-singularity/. Accessed 21 Aug. 2018.

Sokol, B. J., and Mary Sokol. *Shakespeare, Law, and Marriage*. Cambridge UP, 2003.

Soule, Lesley Wade. *Actor as Anti-Character: Dionysus, the Devil, and the Boy Rosalind*. Greenwood Press, 2000.

Suzuki, Tadashi. *Collected Works of Suzuki's Directed Plays and Scripts I: King Lear and Dionysus* (in Japanese). Shizuoka Performing Arts Centre, 2009.

———. *Culture is the Body* (in Japanese and English). Suzuki Company of Toga, 2008.

———. *A Director's Work: Reading Tadashi Suzuki* (in Japanese). Suzuki Company of Toga, 2007.

———. *From Toga to the World: SCOT Summer Season 2009* (in Japanese). Suzuki Company of Toga, 2009.

———. SCOT homepage. http://www.scot-suzukicompany.com/. Accessed 21 Aug. 2018.

———. *What is Theatre?* (in Japanese). Iwanami Shoten, 1988.

Takahashi, Yasunari. "Suzuki's Shakespeare (II): *King Lear*." *The Theatre of Suzuki Tadashi*, written by Ian Carruthers and Yasunari Takahashi, Cambridge UP, 2004, pp. 247-54.

———. "The Work of Tadashi Suzuki in the Context of Japanese Theatre" (in

Japanese). *Suzuki, A Director's Work: Reading Tadashi Suzuki* (in Japanese), Suzuki Company of Toga, 2007, pp. 5-53.

Tan, Marcus Cheng Chye. "Listening in/to Asia: Ong Keng Sen's *Desdemona* and the Polyphonies of Asia." *Acoustic Interculturalism: Listening to Performance*, Palgrave Macmillan, 2012, pp. 133-64.

Tanaka, Nobuko. "World was a stage for acclaimed theatre director Yukio Ninagawa." *Japan Times*, 13 May 2016. http://www.japantimes.co.jp/culture/2016/05/13/stage/world-was-a-stage-for-acclaimed-theater-director-yukio-ninagawa/#.V02aWZGLSUk. Accessed 21 Aug. 2018.

Tawada, Yoko. *Exophony: Travels Outside One's Mother Tongue* (in Japanese). Iwanami Shoten, 2003.

TheatreWorks. *Lear Dreaming*. http://theatreworks.org.sg/international/leardreaming/2012/index.htm. https://theatreworkssg.wordpress.com/tag/lear-dreaming/. Accessed 21 Aug. 2018.

Tiatco, Anril Pineda. "Performance Review of *Lear Dreaming*." *Asian Theatre Journal*, vol. 30, no. 2, Fall 2013, pp. 532-38.

Trivedi, Poonam and Minami Ryuta, editors. *Re-playing Shakespeare in Asia*. Routledge, 2010.

Uchida, Kenshi. "Baptized by Ninagawa Shakespeare." *Higeki Kigeki*, no.780, May 2016, pp. 46-49.

Underground Airport. Homepage. http://www.uga-web.com. Accessed 21 Aug. 2018.

Vogel, Paula. "Desdemona: A Play about a Handkerchief." *Adaptations of Shakespeare: A Critical Anthology of Plays from the Seventeenth Century to the Present*, edited by D. Fischlin and M. Fortier, Routledge, 2000, pp. 233-54.

Watson, Robert N. "Shakespeare's New Words." *Shakespeare Survey*, edited by Peter Holland, vol. 65, Cambridge UP, 2012, pp. 358-77.

Wilson, Richard. *Shakespeare in French Theory: King of Shadows*. Routledge, 2007.

Wilson, Rob and Wimal Dissanayake, editors. *Global/Local: Cultural Production and the Transnational Imaginary*. Duke UP, 1996.

Worthen, W. B. *Shakespeare and the Force of Modern Performance*. Cambridge UP, 2003.

———. *Shakespeare Performance Studies*. Cambridge UP, 2014.

Wright, Laurence. "Interrogating the Spread of Shakespeare." *Multicultural Shakespeare: Translation, Appropriation and Performance,* vol.8, 2012, pp. 5-18.

Yamanote Jijosha. http://www.yamanote-j.org. Accessed 21 Aug. 2018.

Yasuda, Masahiro. "Director's Note," "Programme of *The Tempest.*" Theatre East, Tokyo Metropolitan Theatre, January 2015.

———. "On *The Tempest.*" Personal e-mail. 18 Dec. 2014.

———. "Talk with Yasuda by Manabu Noda and Emi Hamana." *Shūkan Dokushojin* [*Weekly Reader*], 23 May 2014, pp. 4-5.

———. *Yamanote Jijosha 1984-.* Yamanote Jijosha, 2004.

———. "*Yojohan*: Japan is Right There," translated by Kei Hibino and Mao Naito, *Yamanote-Jijosha 1984-*, Yamanote Jijosha, 2004, p. 25.

"Yukio Ninagawa, Theatre Director-Obituary." *The Telegraph.* 26 May 2016. http://www.telegraph.co.uk/obituaries/2016/05/26/yukio-ninagawa-theatre-director-obituary/. Accessed 21 Aug. 2018.

Yong, Li Lan. "Shakespeare and the Fiction of the Intercultural." *A Companion to Shakespeare and Performance,* edited by Barbara Hodgdon and W. B. Worthen, Blackwell, 2007, pp. 527-49.

———. "Shakespeare Here and There: Ong Keng Sen's Intercultural Shakespeare." *Shakespeare in Asia: Contemporary Performance,* edited by Dennis Kennedy and Yong Li Lan, Cambridge UP, 2010, pp. 188-218.

Young, Robert J. C. "That Which Is Casually Called a Language." *PMLA,* vol.131, no.5, 2016, pp. 1207-21.

Zarrilli, Phillip B. "For Whom Is the King a King? Issues of Intercultural Production, Perception, and Reception in a Kathakali *King Lear.*" *Critical Theory and Performance,* edited by Janelle G. Reinelt and Joseph R. Roach, U of Michigan P, 2006, pp. 108-33.

Zeami. *A Mirror Held to the Flower (Kakyō),* translated by J. Thomas Rimer and Yamazaki Masakazu, edited by Daniel Gerould. *Theatre/ Theory/ Theatre: The Major Critical Texts from Aristotle and Zeami to Soyinka and Havel,* Applause, 2000, pp. 106-107.

———. *Performance Notes.* Translated by Tom Hare, Columbia UP, 2011.

List of Original Publications

This book is based on the following original papers, although they have been extensively revised and rewritten for this book. The research for the original publications was supported by Japanese Society for the Promotion of Science Kakenhi (Grant-in-Aid for Scientific Research) 19520193, 23520283, and 26370310.

Chapter 1. "This Is, and Is Not, Shakespeare: A Japanese-Korean Transformation of *Othello*." *Alicante Journal of English Studies / Revista Alicante de Estudio Ingleses*, vol. 25, November 2012, pp. 179-91.

Chapter 2. "Performing Shakespeare in Contemporary Japan: The Yamanote Jijosha's *The Tempest*." *Multicultural Shakespeare: Translation, Appropriation and Performance*, vol.14, no. 1, December 2016, pp. 73-85.

Chapter 3. "Last Shakespeare Plays Directed by Yukio Ninagawa: Possessed by the Power of Theater." *Journal of Literature and Art Studies*, vol. 7, no. 3, March 2017, pp. 269-77.

Chapter 4. "Multilingual Performance of Shakespeare Worldwide: Multilingual *King Lear*, Directed by Tadashi Suzuki as a Case Study." *Shakespeare Special Issue* of *Theatre International*, vol. VII, January 2014, pp. 1-27. NB: The original English paper is an extensively revised version of an earlier Japanese paper on the four-language performance of *King Lear* directed by Suzuki: *Connecting Cultures: From Shakespeare to Contemporary Asian Theatre*, Tsukuba UP, 2012, chapter 6, pp. 103-26.

Chapter 5. "Toward a Study of Translingual Performance of Shakespeare Worldwide with a Focus on Henry V." *Essays and Studies in British and American Literature*, vol. 63, March 2017, pp. 41-64.

Chapter 6. "Translingual Performance of *King Lear: Lear Dreaming* as a Case Study." *Litteraria Pragensia: Studies in Literature & Culture*, vol.26, no. 52, December 2016, pp. 90-105.

Chapter 7. "*Safaring the Night: A Midsummer Night's Dream* Updated." *Shakespeare Studies*, vol. 56, September 2018, pp.18-34.

Appendix. "Review of *Sandaime Richard*, written by Hideki Noda and directed by Ong Keng Sen," *Shakespeare Studies*, vol. 54, March 2017, pp. 40-43.

Author Profile

Emi Hamana, PhD, Professor Emeritus of Tsukuba University, is currently Professor of English Literature at Tokyo Woman's Christian University. She specialises in Shakespeare studies, cultural studies and English Education, focusing on multicultural, multilingual and translingual performances of Shakespeare's plays worldwide, along with intercultural collaboration in contemporary theatre. Her current research interest concerns cognitive and digital approaches to Shakespeare. Her publications include *The Wonder of Gender: Shakespeare and Gender* (in Japanese; Nihon Tosho Centre, 2004) and *Connecting Cultures: From Shakespeare to Contemporary Asian Theatre* (in Japanese; Tsukuba UP, 2012). She has also contributed to *The Cambridge Guide to the Worlds of Shakespeare*, vol. 2 (Cambridge UP, 2016) and *Shakespeare; His Infinite Variety* (Lodz UP, 2017), and to many academic journals. Her website is at https://emihamana.net.

Index

adaptation 8-9, 14-17, 21, 68, 73, 115, 119, 122, 125, 129, 132, 136, 139, 143, 145, 147-148, 150, 154, 159
affect 55-56, 58, 66, 122-123, 126-129, 150, 155-156, 161
all-male Shakespeare series 63
A Midsummer Night's Dream 16, 37, 131-132, 135-137, 139, 143-145, 147-148, 150, 157, 161-162
artificial intelligence (AI) 17, 132-133, 135, 142
Asai, Nobumichi 134, 140
Asian Shakespeare Intercultural Archive (A|S|I|A) 9, 161
Babel 90, 101
Bakhtin, Mikhail 56, 93
cognitive approach 16, 56, 117-118, 123, 129, 131, 151
contact language 15, 94-96
contact zone 15, 75, 89, 94-95, 98
Derrida, Jacques 29-30, 36
digital technology 141, 151
electromagnetic recognition control 135-136, 145
environmental affordance 11, 16, 91, 108, 117
gamelan 16, 115, 125, 155
Gibson, James J. 116, 137

global English 15, 23, 96-97
Globe to Globe 2012 11, 68, 97, 103, 159
Gombrowicz, Witold 38
gut 25-28, 33-34
hanamichi 65
Henry V 15, 89-91, 95-96, 98-99, 102-106, 109, 112-113, 150
heteroglossia 90, 93
heterolingualism 77
Hirakawa, Sukehiro 25, 28-29
immersive theatre 66, 147, 163
intercultural education 8-10
intercultural sensitivity 7-8
interlinguicity 93-94
Ishiguro, Hiroshi 163
Ito, Yasuro 16-17, 131-132, 134, 136-137, 142, 150, 162
Kabuki 62-63, 65, 69, 71, 154-155
King Lear 15-16, 67, 69-74, 77-85, 98, 118, 126, 129, 149-150, 159
Kuo, Pao Kun 75, 77
laser beams 16, 116, 125-128, 160
Lear Dreaming 16, 115, 117-120, 122-123, 125, 128-129, 160-161
Lee, Youn-taek 24-28, 33-35
Lepage, Robert 54
Macbeth 14, 37, 53-54, 60-62
Miyagi, Satoshi 25-29, 32-33, 74

mobile participatory theatre 134, 141, 143
mondialisation 120-122, 154
Morrison, Toni 35
Moscow Art Theatre 70, 72-73
multicultural performance 11, 93
multiculturalism 8, 68, 76, 92
multilingualism 67, 76, 82, 85, 100, 117, 149
Nancy, Jean-Luc 120, 122, 154, 163
National Theatre Wales 132, 134
neuroscience 89, 117, 151
NINAGAWA Macbeth 14, 53, 61-62
Ninagawa, Yukio 14, 24, 53-66, 149, 158-159
Noda, Hideki 153-154, 160, 163
Noh 13, 24-29, 33-34, 38, 69, 71, 78, 118-119, 123-128, 154, 157
Ong, Keng Sen 16, 54, 75, 77, 115, 118-124, 126, 128-129, 131, 150, 153-155, 160-161, 163
Othello 13, 21, 24-29, 31-36, 100, 149, 157-158
the power of theatre 14, 55-56, 62, 66, 159
projection mapping 17, 137, 139-140, 147, 150
real-time multi-ending 143-144
Richard II 14, 53, 57-59, 153-154, 159-160
Safaring the Night 16-17, 131-145, 147-148, 150, 161-163
Sandaime Richard 153-155, 160-161, 163
scenography 16, 56, 58, 117, 129, 134, 155
science fiction 136-139, 141, 145, 147, 162-163

Singapore 16, 54, 68, 75-77, 80-81, 115, 119, 125, 153-154, 160, 163
singularity 17, 132-134, 137, 142, 145, 148, 162
Sir Thomas More 100
site-specific performance 17, 131, 141-143, 147, 150
sublime space 118-119, 126, 128-129
Suzuki Company of Toga (SCOT) 69-70, 77, 80, 159
Suzuki Method of Actor Training 69, 71
Suzuki, Tadashi 15, 24, 67-74, 77-82, 84-85, 149, 159-160
Tawada, Yoko 83-84, 89
The Tempest 13-14, 37, 40-44, 46-48, 50, 136, 141, 149, 158
Theatre Olympics 68, 85
translation 8, 14, 21, 29-31, 34, 41, 53, 55, 71, 74, 76, 81, 83, 89, 91, 93-94, 102, 159-162
translingual imagination 90
translingual performance 10-12, 15-16, 86, 91, 93-94, 113, 118, 122, 129, 131, 139, 147, 149-150, 159
translingual practice 11-12, 15, 86, 89, 91-93, 102, 104, 106, 108-110, 112-113, 118, 150
The Two Gentlemen of Verona 53, 63-66
Underground Airport (UGA) 131-132, 134
virtual reality (VR) 9, 16, 133, 135, 137-138, 142-143, 145, 147-148, 161
Vogel, Paula 35

Yasuda, Masahiro 13-14, 38-43, 46-50
yojohan 38-40, 43-44
Zeami 25, 119, 127-128, 161

浜名恵美（はまな・えみ）

東京都出身。東京女子大学教授、博士（文学）、筑波大学名誉教授。専門はシェイクスピア研究、カルチュラル・スタディーズ、英語教育であり、世界各地で行われているシェイクスピアの多文化、多言語、超言語による上演および現代演劇の異文化コラボレーションに特に注目してきた。現在の研究課題はシェイクスピア上演への認知的アプローチとディジタル・アプローチである。著書は、『ジェンダーの驚き：シェイクスピアとジェンダー』（日本図書センター、2004年）、『文化と文化をつなぐ：シェイクスピアから現代アジア演劇まで』（筑波大学出版会、2012年）他、*The Cambridge Guide to the Worlds of Shakespeare*, vol. 2 (Cambridge UP, 2016) , *Shakespeare; His Infinite Variety* (Lodz UP, 2017)、および多数の学術誌で論文を発表している。ホームページは https://emihamana.net.

Shakespeare Performances in Japan:
Intercultural - Multilingual - Translingual

2019 年 9 月 20 日　初版発行

著者	浜名 恵美 はまな えみ
発行者	三浦衛
発行所	春風社 Shumpusha Publishing Co.,Ltd. 横浜市西区紅葉ヶ丘 53　横浜市教育会館 3 階 〈電話〉045-261-3168　〈FAX〉045-261-3169 〈振替〉00200 1 37524 http://www.shumpu.com　✉ info@shumpu.com
装丁	長田年伸
印刷・製本	シナノ書籍印刷株式会社

乱丁・落丁本は送料小社負担でお取り替えいたします。
©Emi Hamana. All Rights Reserved. Printed in Japan.
ISBN 978-4-86110-657-6 C3098 ¥5500E

＊本書は『東京女子大学学会研究叢書』の一冊として、東京女子大学が、費用の一部を負担し刊行される。